- Renewals are often possible, contact your library.

- Stock can be returned to any Dorset County Library.

DORSET County Council   Dorset County Library HQ, Colliton Park, Dorchester. Dorset DT1 1XJ

SPY IS A DIRTY WORD

Simon Leigh is young, dynamic, wealthy, a self-made man in the true sense. Against his better judgement, Leigh allows himself to be emotionally blackmailed into a strange, new world: a sordid world where, in the chess game of international politics and intrigue, men like Leigh represent the pawns — manoeuvrable and easily dispensable. Spies are not glamour boys. They are faceless, unknown men, doing a difficult and dangerous job. A man does not become a spy: he is made a spy.

RICHARD TEMPLE

◆

SPY IS A
DIRTY WORD

Complete and Unabridged

LINFORD
Leicester

First published in Great Britain in 1970 by
Robert Hale Limited
London

First Linford Edition
published 2004
by arrangement with
Robert Hale Limited
London

British Library CIP Data

Temple, Richard
  Spy is a dirty word.—Large print ed.—
Linford mystery library
  1. Spy stories
  2. Large type books
  I. Title
  823.9′14 [F]

  ISBN 1–84395–574–1

Published by
F. A. Thorpe (Publishing)
Anstey, Leicestershire

Set by Words & Graphics Ltd.
Anstey, Leicestershire
Printed and bound in Great Britain by
T. J. International Ltd., Padstow, Cornwall

This book is printed on acid-free paper

'Let not Death toast his
conquering power
She'll rise a star that fell a flower.'

1

Dinner Invitation

Simon Leigh pressed the buzzer on his desk. 'Janine, will you ask Mr Joyce to come in for a minute, please.'

Leigh sat back in the hard swivel chair and closed his eyes. He had been working under intense pressure and felt mentally exhausted. His secretary's voice over the intercom cut short the movement of relaxation.

'Mr Joyce for you, sir.'

'Send him in, Janine.' Leigh lit a long cigar and exhaled the smoke slowly. The door opened and a man in a white overall entered the office. Leigh looked up and smiled.

'Hello, Donald, come in.'

As Joyce crossed the room, he noted with concern the lines of fatigue beneath Leigh's eyes.

Leigh looked across the broad desk at

the man who was more a trusted friend than an employee. He gestured for him to sit down.

'Donald, while I'm away you'll be looking after things; I have complete confidence in you, but if there's anything you want to discuss with me, now's your chance.'

'Everything's clear enough, Mr Leigh, but with the Swedish order, we'll need another five Design Draughtsmen to work on the Data Logging Machines.'

'How much will they cost us a year?' Leigh asked.

Joyce scratched his head before replying.

'The best part of £2,000 each.'

Leigh jotted down some figures on the pad in front of him.

'You'll have to manage with four, Donald. Think you can do it?'

Joyce smiled. 'We'll have to, sir.'

★ ★ ★

Donald Joyce had been with Leigh since the beginning. A small, cheerful man with a brilliant, technological brain, he had not forgotten the little factory in the East End where Simon Leigh, in the face of ridicule and fierce competition had put into practice the idea that had developed on a trip to the United States. Joyce thought back to the advertisement in the Personal Column of *The Times* which had first brought him into contact with Leigh.

'I am looking for a creative Technologist with experience in the Computer Production field; the successful candidate will face an immense initial challenge and subsequently prosper with a dynamic new Company. Capacity for hard work and a thorough technical knowledge of the computer industry is more important than qualifications.'

Joyce had been intrigued to see what sort of person these days would judge a man on his capabilities and experience rather than on some scrap of paper. He had answered the advertisement.

Dear Sir,

I have read with interest your advertisement in the Personal Column of *The Times* of today's date.

Since leaving Technical College some years ago, I have worked with computers and business machines in both a design and production capacity.

I was recently made redundant by my firm (the largest in this field in Britain) when a change of policy dictated that anyone without the necessary degrees etc., was quote 'of no further service to the Company in an increasingly competitive and broadening field where it is essential to have the very best that the Country can produce.'

If you feel I could be of any service to you, perhaps you would be kind enough to contact me at the above address.

Yours faithfully,

What Joyce did not know was that out of nearly thirty replies to the advertisement, his had been the only one which had really interested Leigh.

The advertisement had not lied, the Company had, indeed, prospered and Joyce with it. He was now Production Manager of a sizeable factory, responsible only to Leigh. He worshipped the man and when he overheard staff discussing Leigh's alleged ruthlessness he would go berserk. There was no room for kid gloves in business, especially in a business where you had to fight, and fight hard for every order.

★　★　★

The 70 mile an hour speed limit did not suit Simon Leigh. To be more accurate, it did not suit his Bristol. To restrict a car like that to 70 miles an hour, was like asking a thoroughbred race horse not to exceed a canter.

Leigh looked in his wing mirror, the outside lane was clear. He pushed his foot down hard on the accelerator, the automatic gears changed down and the car surged forward. The needle on the speedometer flickered near the 100 figure as the gears changed up again into top. Leigh had always maintained that he would never drive an automatic. 'takes all the joy out of driving' he used to say, but now he would never revert to manual gears. 'I must be getting lazy or old, or both,' he thought.

The car was steady as a rock at 110 miles an hour. A sports car was coming very fast towards Leigh down the opposite lane of the motorway; when it was closer he saw that it was a police car and reluctantly slowed to 70. He was amazed at the variety and extent of models the Police now had at their disposal. He had seen a policeman in an Aston Martin booking a girl for speeding a few days previously — '£4,000 of the tax payers money on one car'.

Leigh loved this stretch of the M.4. between the Air port and London, but lately either through road reconstruction work or increased pre-summer traffic, he had been unable to open up the Bristol for any length of time — he had left his factory at Windsor at five o'clock, an hour earlier than usual. He was flying to

Brussels in the morning on the first leg of a sales trip to Belgium and East Germany. As he slowed to come off the motorway he reflected that although the Belgians had begun to manufacture their own business machines and basic computers, they were very much inferior to the ones that his company had developed over nine problematic years and was successfully exporting to a dozen countries including the States. As for the East Germans, the man from E.C.G.D.[1] had predicted that after they had given him the usual bull about their machines being superior to his or anyone elses that they should place a useful initial order.

Over the Hammersmith fly-over Leigh found himself stuck behind a B.E.A. coach which he was not able to overtake until it pulled into the Air Terminal at Cromwell Road. He turned right into Queensberry Place and was parked in the little mews opposite his flat five minutes later. His flat was in a modern block off

---

[1] E.C.G.D. Export Credits Guarantee Department of the British Government.

Sloane Square and judging by the cars that were parked outside and the people he met coming in and out, was largely inhabited by Arab playboys or 'diplomats' as they liked to call themselves.

Leigh's flat was on the ninth floor, one from the top. 'They should do something about speeding up this lift' he thought, as he did each time he used it. He had lived here since his wife had been killed in a car accident four years earlier, just five months after they had been married. It would have been senseless for him to have kept up the large house in Regents Park; they had bought it for the children they were going to have, and for the entertaining that Klaire used to tease him was so essential for a budding tycoon. Leigh did no entertaining in his flat, but took any business colleagues out to restaurants and clubs.

He poured himself a large whisky and turned on the television for the six o'clock news —

Jordan and Israel had been exchanging mortar fire again across the border.

Four dead on each side.

Leigh could not see peace lasting very long in the Middle East. There was too much hate and tension.

He was pouring another drink when the telephone rang.

'Hello.'

'Hello, Simon. Peter here. How are you?'

'Fine, Peter, and you?'

'Very well.'

★ ★ ★

Peter Gorebain was one of Leigh's few friends. They had fought together in Korea in the Commandos, and had struck up a friendship which, unlike many war time associations, had lasted. They did not see a great deal of each other now, perhaps half a dozen times a year, but this seemed to strengthen rather than weaken the bond between them.

★ ★ ★

'Simon, I was wondering whether you would like to have dinner with me this evening. I know it's short notice, but I'd be delighted if you could make it.'

'It's nice of you, Peter, but I'm leaving for the Continent in the morning, and I really have a lot to do before I go.'

'It won't be a late night, old boy, it seems ages since we've seen each other.'

Leigh could think of no convincing reason why he should not have dinner with Peter Gorebain and he accepted the invitation.

'Good. Meet you in the Dorchester bar at 8.30. Bye.'

Leigh showered and changed into a dark grey suit, white silk shirt and wide blue tie. He was not a vain man, but he took a great deal of trouble over his appearance because he thought it important. As he straightened his tie, he surveyed himself critically in the bathroom mirror. He saw a dark, tall man, who, thanks to a weekly game of squash, still had a good figure — a little on the thin side, if anything. A lean face with large green eyes, and a wide almost sensual mouth stared back at him. His hair still damp, looked blacker than it really was. Women found the unusual contrast between his eyes and hair attractive. There were wrinkles at the corners of his eyes which he had not noticed before, but he optimistically put these down to overwork, and not age. His naturally cold expression lent him a hard, insensitive air. He shrugged at his reflection and left the flat.

Leigh decided to walk to the Dorchester. Being cooped up in an office all day was no good to anyone. 'I'm becoming like all the millions of other car bound Londoners', he reflected as he walked through Belgrave Square enjoying the fresh evening air and fast falling darkness.

As he walked, he realized not for the first time how much he was looking forward to his forthcoming trip; he had not had a break from the factory for a long time. 'Perhaps if everything goes well, I will extend the trip into a short vacation and go from East Berlin to Paris or Rome'. But then the cloud descended as it always did when Simon Leigh's thoughts turned to any form of break from his work. 'What will I do in Paris or Rome on my own? I might just as well stay in London.' Moodily he kicked a small stone lying on the pavement: he watched it scud off the kerb into the gutter.

Leigh turned his thoughts back to his business. A few months previously a large American Corporation had made a very tempting offer to buy him out, but he had turned them down and had no regrets. Simon Leigh's philosophy towards business was simple — once a certain stage of money making is reached, the money itself is no longer important. It is the creative side of the business, the growing from strength to strength that becomes the vital factor, the driving force. Every penny Leigh had made had been earned by sweat and toil. He had made it a lot faster than many men, but this was because he had launched his business when there were unfulfilled demands for the products he manufactured and he had grown with the demand. Leigh exercised a rigid control over the money in his business, taking excessive pains to ensure that not a penny was unnecessarily wasted.

But with his private, personal money, it was a different story. To many men, money becomes the master and they derive no pleasure from their years of hard work. Leigh was determined that this should not happen to him. He was generous and impulsive with his private money: too impulsive sometimes as he had discovered to his bitter cost.

That never to be forgotten summer evening four years before was as clear in his mind as if it had been last night. As he crossed Hyde Park Corner by the underpass Leigh remembered the look of pleasure and disbelief on Klaire's face when he had handed her a set of car keys on her twenty-sixth birthday.

'The car's outside,' he had said. Klaire rushed over to the window and looked out. Below on the opposite side of the road was parked the metallic silver 'E' Type Jaguar that Leigh had seen in the Piccadilly car showroom four days before. He had gone in and the slick young salesman had spent twenty minutes extolling the car's virtues.

'A real beauty, sir. Grace, space, pace as they say in the advertisement. Only done five thousand miles since new. One lady owner — gather she found it a bit too fierce: but for you, sir, just the job.'

'It's not for me,' Leigh had said with a slight smile. 'It's for my wife.' He had written out the cheque there and then.

Klaire had insisted that they drive somewhere that same evening and he had suggested that they go to Skindles for dinner.

'You drive, darling,' she had said after thoroughly examining her new toy. 'I'll have all the time in the world to drive her.'

Leigh had touched 130 miles an hour on the motorway but when he saw Klaire's look of delight as she watched the speedometer flickering further and further round the dial he had slowed down, and had warned her against following his example when driving herself.

'There's a big difference between this and your Mini Cooper, darling; get used to it slowly before trying to break the land speed record!' he said, as he turned into the car park at Skindles. He knew that his words would have little effect on her, but she was an excellent driver and he was not really worried. She had laughed at his concern and had kissed him.

It was a warm evening and they had sat on the terrace overlooking the river. There was a large traffic in small pleasure boats and canoes. They took a long time over the meal and when they had finished Simon asked Klaire if she would like him to hire a boat for an hour or two.

'No, sweetie. Lets take the hood down on the car. That'll be much better than a boat. It's ages since I've felt the wind roaring in my face.'

It had taken him a few minutes to get the hood down. 'Sure you don't want to drive, darling?'

'No, it makes me feel good to be driven by handsome men in fast cars!'

'What do you mean, men?' he had asked in mock seriousness.

'I mean you, Simon.'

He had driven slowly out of Maidenhead enjoying, with Klaire, the admiring glances of all who saw the car. On the motorway he held her at 80 miles an hour enjoying the feeling of reserve power under his foot, the cool night air rushing past his face.

'Doesn't that long, silver bonnet look fabulous?' shouted Klaire above the noise of the engine and wind.

Leigh nodded and turned briefly to look at her. Her long blonde hair was flapping around her face and in the dark he could just make out tears from the wind in her high-spirited eyes. She smiled at him and squeezed his hand which was resting lightly on the steering wheel.

'I must remind Klaire about renewing her licence when we get home.' Leigh thought, accelerating round a slight bend in the road.

The next few moments he had never been able to recall in detail although he had gone over them hundreds of times in his mind. A pair of headlights undipped and blinding had come flashing across the centre verge of the motorway. Leigh tried to swerve but it was too late. There was a sickening marriage of metal against metal, an explosion, and the next thing he remembered was lying on his back on the hard tarmac surrounded by policemen. His back hurt terribly but he managed, with the help of two constables, to stagger to his feet. Blood was oozing from a cut on his forehead and his voice seemed strange and foreign to him.

'My wife,' he screamed. 'In the car.' He attempted to walk to the mangled remains of the Jaguar which had come to rest on the grass verge but two policemen stopped him.

'She's been taken away in an ambulance, sir. There's nothing you can do now.'

A few yards from the wreckage of the Jaguar was another car, so badly distorted that its make was totally unrecognizable.

Leigh shook himself free of the policemen and vomited twice.

'I think we'd better get you to hospital too, sir.'

Leigh heard two men standing by his car, discussing the accident. 'Miracle that he was thrown clear,' said one.

The other nodded. 'It's often the case with these convertibles. One's thrown clear and the other's trapped in the car.'

As the policemen tried to help him towards the ambulance he again wrenched himself free from their grasp.

'Don't want any bloody hospital — see my wife — her car — birthday present — she . . . ' Leigh fainted.

It had been the doctor who had broken the news to Leigh. He had been taken to the same hospital as Klaire and as soon as he came round, he demanded to know what had happened to his wife. It was one o'clock in the morning and the doctor, who had not been to bed for thirty-six hours, sat at Leigh's bedside. He quickly sized up the man lying in the bed and knew that the truth would be the only way.

'I'm sorry.' Mr Leigh, but your wife was dead before she was put into the ambulance, it must have been very quick. The police say there was nothing you could have done to prevent it. An old man fell asleep at the wheel of his car and

18

it veered over from the other side of the motorway and crashed into yours; he died too, I am afraid.'

As he walked up Park Lane towards the Dorchester, Simon Leigh forced these bitter memories out of his mind, and quickened his step.

2

Old Friends, New Friends

The American bar at the Dorchester was, as always, crowded with a cocktail of show business personalities, businessmen continuing their negotiations from the boardroom and foreign visitors. Leigh stood by the bar and looked around. Gorebain was sitting in a corner talking to a short bald man in a shiny mohair suit. Leigh seemed to recognize the man's face which had the flabbiness of too much good living coupled with little or no exercise.

He walked over to the table and Gorebain stood up and held out his hand. Gorebain was a bachelor and many people thought he was queer. Leigh had never found any evidence to support this. He was some sort of Civil Servant in the Admiralty, but unlike many of his colleagues was not in the least stuffy or conceited.

'Good to see you, Simon, you're looking well. Do you know Harold Levenson?'

Leigh had not met Levenson before, but now remembered him from his not infrequent appearances on the city page of the newspapers. His original business had been property but he had so diversified his activities since, that if anyone ever asked him what business he was in, he would merely shrug his shoulders and say, 'I'm in the 'business' business.'

Leigh shook hands with him and sat down.

'What are you drinking, Mr Leigh?' asked Levenson, in a surprisingly cultured voice.

'Johnnie Walker Black Label and Apollinaris, please.'

'Make it a double,' Levenson told the hovering waiter.

'You don't take ice do you, Mr Leigh?' asked the waiter.

'No thanks, Jimmy.' Leigh did not come here much now, but when Klaire had been alive it had been one of their favourite drinking spots especially on Sunday mornings, when the bar assumed the character of a private club with the same familiar faces reappearing week after week.

Almost immediately, Levenson excused himself to make a telephone call.

'I hope you don't mind, Simon,' said Gorebain when he had gone, 'but I've asked Levenson to join us for dinner.'

'Not at all,' said Leigh, who was disappointed as this would mean that Peter and he could not catch up on the various items of news interesting only to themselves, which they invariably discussed when they met.

'I thought he would be a useful man for you to know,' continued Gorebain. 'You never know when someone like that is going to prove an asset. He has a finger in so many pies.'

'I didn't know you moved in such elevated business circles,' smiled Leigh, half teasing, half questioning. Gorebain made some trite response and the matter passed.

Leigh was genuinely surprised that Gorebain knew Levenson and appeared to be on such friendly terms with him. The two men were totally different in character, had on the surface so little in common.

'Well, Simon, what have you been up to since we last met? When am I coming for a cruise on the yacht?'

Leigh laughed. A few years before, he had toyed with the idea of buying a yacht; he had gone so far as to have some designs drawn up by a firm of boat builders that Gorebain had unofficially recommended to him, but after his wife's death he had lost interest in the idea, and nothing had come of it. Whenever they met, Gorebain would mention it.

Leigh smiled as he remembered the playful arguments he had had with Klaire over where the yacht should be moored. He had wanted to keep it at Poole so that they could make use of it at week-ends to sail to Cherbourg or the Channel Islands, but Klaire, who was a sun worshipper, had insisted that they keep it in Cannes or some other Mediterranean port.

'We can fly out at week-ends, sleep on the boat and fly back bronzed and beautiful on Monday morning,' she had suggested in her adorable but sometimes impractical way.

'It rains in Cannes too,' Leigh had said.

But she had scathingly shot this argument to the ground with, 'Well, I'd rather have the South of France rain than the British.'

Gorebain's voice brought him back to the present. 'You know, Simon, it would do you good to have a yacht — something to look forward to at week-ends, something to take your mind off your business. Honestly, old boy, you'll have an ulcer before you're forty.' Gorebain knew that Leigh invariably worked right through the weekend.

Leigh finished his drink and lit a long Dutch Panatella. 'What the hell do I want to go sailing off at week-ends on my own for?' he asked, annoyed with himself for being angry with Gorebain who he knew had his best interests at heart.

'I could give you the obvious answer to

that, Simon, but I won't. Have another drink.'

Gorebain was one of the few people who knew how badly Klaire's death had affected Simon Leigh. Leigh was an undemonstrative man, but he felt things deeply nonetheless. Gorebain had been with him in the few days immediately following the accident and he had behaved absolutely as normal; in fact, Gorebain remembered a number of people who had not known Leigh well remarking how unfeeling and heartless a man he must be to take his wife's death so casually, but Gorebain knew that nothing could have been further from the truth. Only once had he seen Simon let the mask slip. He had gone with him to place flowers on Klaire's grave one Sunday afternoon, a year after her death. Leigh had knelt on the hard earth and with a bitterness that Gorebain did not recognize, had whispered in an unsteady voice: 'I wish to God I could have died with you, darling.'

Although in his day to day life Leigh did not betray his unhappiness, he had for a while, taken to gambling with a regularity and recklessness that had frightened Gorebain; but Leigh was not the sort of man you could talk to and Gorebain had prayed that Leigh, who had always taken gambling seriously, would ease off and return to the card tables as a recreation rather than a necessity. Once when Klaire was still alive, Gorebain had asked him why he enjoyed gambling so much — the money was no longer important.

Leigh had thought for a moment before replying, 'I gamble purely for pleasure, the way some men play tennis or go fishing. Every day I'm faced with problems and worries in my business. When I sit down at a card table I exchange these day to day worries for a more imminent, temporarily more serious set of worries. This is my form of relaxation, my way of escaping.'

This Gorebain could understand, but the gambling Leigh had adopted after Klaire's death was a different proposition to the relaxation Leigh spoke of, with hundreds and occasionally thousands of pounds being won and lost in a night. But gradually he had eased off and one evening, after a particularly large win, Leigh had not gambled again for three months, and when he did return to the tables, it was the old Leigh, cool and calculating that had taken the place of the reckless, 'don't care if I lose' Leigh of the past months.

★　★　★

Levenson returned from his telephone call apologizing for being away so long. The conversation turned to the investment potential of paintings. Harold Levenson had a distinguished and valuable private art collection, and he enjoyed nothing more than to let slip none too discreetly how much he had paid for a certain painting and how much that painting was now worth. Leigh for some reason that he could not rationalize had taken an instinctive dislike to the plump millionaire who purchased Old Masters the way most men bought cigarettes.

After the fourth round of drinks

Gorebain looked at his watch.

'We ought to think about dinner. I've booked a table at Parkes for 9.30.'

The three men drove to the restaurant in Levenson's black Bentley. On the short drive from Park Lane to Beauchamp Place, Levenson asked Leigh about his business. Leigh answered his questions factually and without embellishment. He told Levenson of the percentage increase in turnover and profits in the six years since he had started the Company.

The industrialist seemed impressed and said, 'The computer field is one of the few that I have no experience of. Of course your business must be a very specialized one to be able to compete with the big boys like Elliott and I.C.L.'

'It is,' agreed Leigh. 'I only employ 250 people but the machines we manufacture would not be big enough in terms of production runs for the larger concerns, so there is, in fact, little direct competition with them.'

Over the excellent dinner, they continued to discuss Leigh's business and he was delighted to be able to talk about it to two men who appeared genuinely interested. He had, of necessity, kept all his achievements, failures, problems and hopes to himself lately, and it was refreshing to be able to discuss these things again with a man of Levenson's reputation and proven ability and Gorebain with whom he usually never discussed his business other than to make the occasional general comment.

After the meal Gorebain, who only smoked cigarettes, was about to order cigars for his guests, but Levenson stopped him.

'Let Simon try one of these.' He took from his breast pocket a crocodile skin cigar case and handed it to Leigh who extracted one of the fat torpedo-shaped cigars; it was deep brown in colour and had green spots down the length of it, there was no band.

'I have them rolled specially for me in Cuba and conditioned at Dunhills,' Levenson explained.

Leigh cut the cigar with his silver cutter and lit it, inhaling the rich mellow smoke slowly to the back of his throat — he exhaled slowly. It was a superb cigar and he told Levenson, who seemed pleased and lit his own; he declined the offer of Leigh's cutter, piercing his cigar carefully with a wooden match.

After Gorebain had asked for the bill Levenson invited them both back to his flat for a nightcap.

'It's very nice of you, but I really do have to be up early in the morning,' said Leigh, 'and if I drink much more, I won't get up at all!'

'One drink won't hurt,' protested Gorebain. 'And I know Harold's dying to show us his latest Picasso.'

Because he did not want to hurt Gorebain's feelings when the man had obviously taken a great deal of trouble to arrange the meeting between him and Levenson, Leigh reluctantly accepted the invitation.

'Splendid,' said Levenson. And after Gorebain had paid the bill the three men walked up the steps of the restaurant into the cool Knightsbridge air.

Levenson's penthouse flat occupied the

whole top floor of an enormous block behind Park Lane. The lift opened straight into his hall. Levenson and his wife were separated but throughout the flat evidence of her taste was present. She was a well known interior decorator and the flat was the mixture of antique and modern which, ideal in theory, rarely succeeds in practice, but Leigh could not fault her taste.

Levenson led the way to the 'gallery' as he called the high-ceilinged room where he kept his paintings. Leigh was amazed by the extent and beauty of his collection. On three walls were hung Rubens, Gauguins, Rembrandts, and the latest acquisition, an early Picasso. The fourth wall was hung completely with prints of children of all ages and Levenson explained that he had a special fondness for child prints. Each painting had an individual light over it and it would have taken a good hour for Leigh to study the collection in detail.

Levenson led the way back to the study which adjoined the sitting-room and opening a bottle of Martell Cordon Bleu filled three balloon shaped brandy glasses.

'Simon,' said Levenson when the three men were comfortably installed in arm-chairs, pale blue smoke from their cigars sending a misty haze up to the four nymph wall lights which adorned the panelled walls, 'I have a confession to make.'

Leigh looked at Levenson to see if he was about to make a joke but the expression on his fleshy face remained serious.

'I asked Peter to arrange this meeting between us tonight.'

Leigh looked at Gorebain who was staring thoughtfully at the glass in his hand. Leigh was realistic and he knew that a man like Levenson would not spend a whole evening discussing another man's business without some good motive. He waited for the proposition to materialize.

'I had an ulterior motive,' continued Levenson slowly, tapping his cigar gently on the cut glass ashtray to rid it of ash. He looked intently at Leigh and took a sip from the balloon glass in his hand.

Then as if making a decision he put the glass down, stood up and walked to the large antique desk in the corner of the room where he stood facing his two guests, his hands clasped behind his back.

'Simon, you have told us tonight something of your business activities and this confirms my original assessment and opinion that in you we had a man of intelligence, initiative and experience far beyond his years.' Leigh did not know how to take this remark and remained silent. Gorebain continued to gaze at his untouched brandy.

'You're a man who appreciates straight talking,' Levenson went on, 'and I'll not put a sugar coating on the pill I'm going to offer you. You leave tomorrow for Belgium; from there I understand you will be going on to East Germany.'

Leigh frowned and looked sharply at Levenson and then at Gorebain who glanced up briefly. He had mentioned over dinner that he was going to Brussels but he had had no occasion to discuss any other details of his trip and had certainly not mentioned he would be visiting East Germany.

The atmosphere in the room, which five minutes previously had been full of bonhomie and humour, was now inexplicably tension-filled and uncomfortable. Leigh waited with no pleasure for what was to come. It was certainly not going to be the type of proposition he had anticipated.

Levenson smiled. 'I understand from Peter that you are a gambler. Well, Simon, I'm going to offer you a gamble where the stakes are higher than in any casino, and the winnings are infinitely more worthwhile.'

'In that case,' said Leigh, his face hard and unsmiling, 'let's talk about the odds.'

3

The Gentle Art of Persuasion

'I must have been drunk,' thought Leigh, knowing that he had never been more sober in his life. He looked out of the Caravelle porthole at the clouds gently floating over the English Channel.

He had not left Levenson's flat until three and had been unable to sleep for the brief remainder of the night. He wondered why he was not feeling tired this morning.

The Captain's voice over the cabin speaker interrupted his thoughts. 'Ladies and Gentlemen, we will be landing at Brussels airport in ten minutes. I hope that you have enjoyed the flight and will have a pleasant stay in Belgium.'

Leigh extinguished his Panatella and when the pretty stewardess with the slightly plump face came to see that everybody had fastened their seat belts, he clasped his hands over the two loose ends of the belt so that they looked fastened. He hated being restricted and never fastened the seat belts either in his car or in an aeroplane. If he was going to die he did not believe that the nylon belt across his stomach would save him.

It was cold in Brussels and the sky was overcast and foreboding. Leigh turned up the collar of his overcoat as he walked across the tarmac towards the customs building.

The driver of the Opel taxi which Leigh hired to take him to his hotel did not stop talking for one minute of the drive from the airport. He was a short, stocky man with an aggressive black moustache and dirty teeth. He wore a blue anorak and tight green corduroy trousers.

'You know my sister?' he asked in French the moment Leigh entered the cab. 'She lives in Leeds, her name is Mrs Scott. Her husband is a very important man on the Council.'

Leigh said that regrettably he had not had the pleasure of meeting the man's sister, but the driver was not in the least put out and shaking his fist at an innocent cyclist whom he narrowly missed knocking over, proceeded to reel off a seemingly endless list of relations and friends living in England, and at each name he would mention the town in which the particular person lived and ask if Leigh knew them.

Leigh gave an audible sigh of relief when the car finally pulled up with a dramatic screech of brakes at the Palace Hotel. He greatly overtipped the driver, so grateful was he to have escaped the man's relations and friends. The driver shook Leigh's hand vigorously and promised to come and see him when he came to England to visit his relatives. As he was driving off, he leaned out of the window and shouted after Leigh:

'Hey, where do you live, Monsieur, so I'll know where to find you?'

'London,' replied Leigh.

'Good,' shouted the man. 'I'll come and see you. Au revoir.'

Last night, although only hours away seemed unreal and artificial to Leigh as he unpacked his large Revelation in his room at the Palace Hotel. With the midday sun which had suddenly appeared, casting a shadow over the pale grey carpet and a church bell chiming somewhere nearby, Levenson, Gorebain and last night were surely a dream — a nightmare. Leigh looked at his faded leather cigar case lying innocently on the bedside table, and the events of the previous night were vividly recalled to his troubled mind.

* * *

Levenson had refilled their three glasses with brandy and had carefully re-lit his cigar with a gold Dupont before continuing.

'Simon, when you have read in the newspapers, as you no doubt have, of men like Abel and Philby, what has been your reaction?'

Levenson gave Leigh no chance to answer but went on, 'When you have read about these men and others like them you have, I am sure, accepted without question that they exist and are not merely figments of some propagandist's colourful imagination. Exist, Simon as spies. Spy is a dirty word when you peel off the layer of glamour which seems to surround it nowadays. But spies are real people; people who do what they have to do not for glory or money, and believe me, the pay is very mediocre. They do what they have to do to try and make their country a safer or at least a slightly less dangerous place in which to live. Spies are a necessary evil and all nations of any size have them. Obviously the more powerful countries have more efficient and numerous agents than those countries with little to hide or protect.'

Levenson took a sip of his brandy and wiped his forehead with a silk handkerchief before continuing. 'I have given you this very brief account of spies, Simon, so that when I ask you what I am going to ask, you will understand that I am talking about normal human beings — men like you and I who have headaches and go to the lavatory and feel depressed sometimes. Not debonair playboys with beautiful blonde assistants and flashy cars.'

To hear Levenson the respected industrialist and art collector speak of these
things so earnestly and with such fervour
shocked Leigh. Also with the first real
foretaste of what was to come, his
stomach muscles knotted and he felt
momentarily cold and shivery.

Before he could begin to sort out his
conflicting thoughts, Gorebain, who until
now had not said a word, looked up.
'Harold, before you go on, perhaps I
could say a few words.'

Levenson returned to his chair and
gestured for Gorebain to carry on.
Gorebain did not stand up but looked
across at Leigh.

'Simon,' he began, 'we know each other
well and I think you know I would not
deliberately deceive you about anything
unless there was an absolutely essential
reason why I should have to. You must be
thinking that I have behaved abominably
to invite you to dinner and then confront
you with this.'

Leigh who had also remained silent
throughout Levenson's speech thought it
time that he said something. 'I would

point out, Peter, that I don't yet know what it is that I am confronted with, but from what Harold has been saying, I certainly don't like it and don't particularly want to know.'

Gorebain made no comment to this but continued, 'Simon, you will have to know that my Admiralty job is a cover, a legitimate cover, for all the administration and field control of all British Agents operating in certain Soviet Satellites of which East Germany is one. My work is also concerned with the recruitment, training and infiltration of these agents. Every year a number of them are caught or disappear without trace, which amounts to the same thing. Finding new personnel of the right calibre to replace them is becoming an increasingly more difficult task. We are dependent more and more on 'part time' agents who do one mission and then 'rest' for a while. They don't do anything else for us for perhaps a year or more. This method has its advantages in that they are never with us long enough at any one time for the other side to mark them down which happens with most of our regular field agents, but on the other hand they are not so highly trained and practised as the others so the risk of their being caught is increased. For the past few years, my department has kept its eye on you along with several other ex-commando officers. You have been annually processed and judging by the reports I have had, you are of the right calibre and temperament for this type of work.'

Leigh now made no attempt to hide his feelings. He stood up, his face white with rage. 'My God,' he shouted, making no attempt to control his voice. 'Know thy friends. I don't bloody well know you do I Peter . . . '

'Sit down please, Simon,' said Levenson quietly. 'Losing your temper will not be of the slightest benefit to anybody. You must realize there are certain things that come even before friendship.'

Leigh turned his enraged mind on to Levenson whose fleshy face was expressionless. 'Mr Levenson, I don't know a great deal about you, other than from what I have read, but whatever your tie-up is in this business, it has nothing to do with what I have to say to Peter. This man was my friend, more than a friend. A man I trusted implicitly. A man who during Korea and after I respected more than anybody. Someone who I could rely on utterly and completely — to find now that he has been using me all these years, using our friendship, so that he could 'annually process me' whatever that means.'

'I think you are taking a slightly melodramatic view, Simon,' said Levenson. 'Peter has done nothing to reproach himself for and no one is using you — yet. Hear us out before you start making snap judgement and drawing false conclusions.'

'No, Harold,' Gorebain interrupted. 'Simon has a right to be angry, but I think when he has heard more, he will be able to understand.' Now it was Gorebain's turn to stand up. He pushed a lock of hair which had fallen on to his forehead back into place and turned to face Leigh.

'Simon, do you remember those nights in the stinking swamps when we were

43

under constant fire and attack by the North Koreans, how we both agreed it would be preferable to be dead than be captured by them? Well, we're still fighting; it's a different kind of war now and a different enemy, but we're still fighting for the same objective — freedom and the right to live in peace — freedom, not just for us but for future generations. The outcome if we lose would be as bad as if we had lost either of the world wars, worse probably. This is a war where the machine guns have been replaced by cipher machines and the soldiers by agents or spies. It is not an open war and most people don't even realize its going on and if they do they turn their minds away from it. After all it doesn't affect them, there's no rationing, no air-raid warnings, no mass evacuation, but believe me, Simon, it's as much a war as the one we fought together in the filth and sweat and humidity of the Korean quagmires.'

Gorebain's face was damp with perspiration and his usual quiet manner was replaced by the man who clamped his hand roughly on Leigh's shoulder and said, 'Harold is right, I have nothing to reproach myself for, Simon, nothing. Just now you talked to me as if we had ceased to be friends. This, I hope, is not so. You must understand that just as in the war we had to forget the individual for the good of the whole platoon, so I have had to put my duty before my friendship to you. I know that if you really think about this you'll see that however unpleasant it may seem, this is the way it has to be.'

Leigh felt confused and out of his depth. It was as if the Peter Gorebain he had known for fifteen years had been replaced by another man with the same outward appearance, but a man he did not know as a person at all.

Levenson cleared his throat. 'I will proceed now, Peter.' Gorebain nodded and sat down.

Leigh looked from Gorebain to Levenson and back again then he, too, returned to his chair — his face still pale.

'Simon,' Levenson began, 'I'd like you to let me finish before you say anything. I know it has shocked you to see Peter and myself, to a lesser extent, revealed in so different a light to the one to which you are accustomed, but I would ask you to bear with me until I have finished.

'There's no reason why you should have to know at this stage exactly where I fit into the picture. Suffice it to say that I'm 'Chairman' of the organization of which Peter is one of the 'Executive Directors'. Just now, Peter talked of a war, he was not exaggerating. Every day men are killed in it, not in hundreds, not openly, but nevertheless they are killed, usually very unpleasantly.

'We want you, Simon, to join our 'army' for the duration of your trip to Europe. To do your bit to help protect Britain and the people in it. To do your job as you did unhesitatingly and naturally in Asia. There will be no tangible reward, no recognition, but we would not ask this of you if it was not absolutely vital.'

Leigh sat back and put down his glass. He felt completely calm and rational now.

'So far,' he said softly, 'I have done all the listening. Well, now I want you both to listen to me.

'I'm not,' he went on speaking very slowly, 'going to be conned into any bloody James Bond escapade unless I know exactly what is involved. So far you have tried to emotionally blackmail me with patriotism and conscience, but unless you tell me everything and I understand one hundred per cent what is at stake, you can find yourself another lemon.

'I'm a businessman trying desperately hard to break into the export markets of Europe. I'm beginning to succeed and I don't see why I should jeopardize these chances, regardless of any personal considerations, without a damned good idea of what I'm letting myself in for.'

Levenson studied Leigh carefully. He learned a great deal from people by studying their faces especially their eyes and looking into this man's eyes he knew that in Leigh he had a dangerous man. A man who properly motivated could and would be of the greatest benefit to the Secret Service.

★　★　★

In Brussels the sun had gone in, only to be replaced by a slow depressing drizzle. Leigh finished unpacking and rang down to room service.

'Send me up a bottle of Johnnie Walker Black Label and a packet of Schimmelpenninck cigars.

'No, no ice.' Leigh went over to the window and watched the rain falling with disgust. He had never liked Brussels, the weather was too much like London, but the city lacked London's charm and character.

4

Kill Two Birds

The General controlled the East German Secret Service from a luxurious suite of offices occupying the top two floors of the Ministry of Trade. He had at his disposal the vast resources of the Soviet Intelligence Service, the K.G.B., and did not hesitate to make use of them whenever necessary. Unlike Britain whose M.I.6 and M.I.5 are individually concerned, the one with counter espionage abroad and the other internal security and counter espionage at home, the General ran the Intelligence Service of East Germany as a single entity with a number of off-spring and sub-divisions.

His official Government title was Administrator and Co-ordinator of Foreign Trade Promotion which was a cover known to every intelligence chief in the West, but which the General retained to enable him to openly meet visiting members of delegations and trade fairs, the most common camouflage for 'part-time' espionage agents. He preferred to assess people himself rather than rely on a subordinate's judgement, and on two occasions his instinctive suspicions of a visiting toy manufacturer from Canada and a respected timber importer from the United States had led to the justifiable arrest of these two 'businessmen' as spies. The General prided himself on his ability to see through a man's outward armour and into his real self. He had a long record of successes in the detection and interrogation of spies and he enjoyed the latter part of his work immensely. There were those who secretly believed that the General's womanising and taste for high living would one day lead him into deep waters with the Party, but the General was a shrewd man and he knew that as long as he continued to do a first class job, his services would not be dispensed with and a blind eye would continue to be turned towards the 'fringe benefits' in which he indulged himself. Also the time was drawing very near when the General would produce his trump card and bring in the British Agents operating under various covers throughout the Republic. It had taken him four long years to gather the information which he and he alone now had stored in his brain: much blood and a great deal of money had been spent in the compiling of this information, but it had been worth it and before long the fruits of these four years would be ripe and ready for plucking. Meanwhile he would do nothing to arouse their suspicions. He would leave them like foxes in an open field unaware of the huntsmen closing in for the kill.

The General pushed aside the folder he had been reading which contained the names and particulars of all foreigners coming to the Republic over the next two months. He picked up the internal black telephone from his ornate Louis XIV desk.

'I'll see Donecke now,' he said and replaced the receiver. Carefully he fitted an oval shaped cigarette into his Ronson Puafilter holder. Soon the clinging aroma of sweet Turkish tobacco enveloped the room. The General inhaled deeply and waited impatiently for his subordinate.

Hans Donecke was the official with the unenviable task of vetting and thereafter having a close watch kept on every foreigner who applied for a visa to visit the German Federal Republic for the first time.

'Why have I not had the report on this Englishman, Simon Leigh, who is coming here next week?' he snapped at Donecke as soon as he entered the room.

'I am sorry, Herr General, but as he was invited by the Department for Foreign Trade Promotion I thought he would have already been cleared.'

'I don't care if he was invited by the Department for Foreign Trade Promotion or Comrade Ulbricht himself!' shouted the General, ejecting a nicotine stained filter from his holder. 'The fact remains that we still have to know something about the man, and he certainly has not been cleared by my Department.'

Donecke sighed as he often did and looked upset. He was a small, mournful man with sparse ginger hair, thin lips and the complexion of a man with ulcers. His suit in strong contrast to the General's crisp, beige uniform was charcoal coloured and clerical. As always, he was wearing heavy brown brogues with steel tips on the heels. The noise he made as he walked along the pavement compensated a little for the lack of authority he held in the Department. People always looked at him and he felt sure they thought him to be a very important man.

The General gestured for Donecke to take a seat and the latter, trying in vain to look unconcerned, crossed the room and sat down.

'Well,' said the General in a less aggressive tone. 'What are we going to do?' He leant over the desk and stared into the man's frightened eyes.

'I don't know, Herr General,' said Donecke miserably. 'We cannot withdraw the visa now. We should look stupid.'

The General who thought Donecke was stupid shook his head sadly as if in the presence of a man for whom he held no hope.

'You idiot,' he suddenly shouted. 'I am not suggesting for one moment that we should withdraw the visa. I am telling you that just because a foreigner from an unfriendly power comes here at our invitation, it does not mean that we can automatically assume that he is clean. On the contrary, we must be more vigilant and careful than ever.' The General lit a fresh cigarette then he shook his head again.

'Get out, Donecke. Get out. Go and promote some trade. As usual it is left to me to do your job for you.'

Gratefully Donecke scurried from the room muttering how sorry he was not to have handled the matter more competently, but the General was already on the phone to his assistant Colonel Muller.

'Adolf, there is a British businessman coming here next week at the invitation of Donecke's department. As usual the little worm has not done his work properly and we know virtually nothing about the man. His name is Leigh, Simon Leigh, and at present he is in Brussels. It struck me that we could kill two birds with one stone

— Suki Laval is in Brussels and she has been idle for far too long.'

'Shall I issue a Personal Dossier, Herr General?' asked Muller, who wore the green uniform he had worn in the Gestapo.

'Yes, make the usual arrangement and bring the order to me for signing, it must go off immediately.'

* * *

The lack of sleep the night before was beginning to affect Simon Leigh. He felt tired and listless. He would have liked to have had an omelette in his room and gone straight to bed, but Paul Davos, the Managing Director of a large electrical concern with whom he hoped to do business had telephoned and asked Leigh to join him and his wife for dinner: it would not have been policy to refuse. After a long, cold shower and two large whiskys, Leigh felt better and more able to face the evening ahead. He was determined to put East Berlin in the back of his mind until he actually arrived there. His thoughts turned again to the previous night.

★ ★ ★

When Levenson had eventually come round to telling him what he had to do, Leigh whose imagination had run riot, had prepared himself for anything — passing information, receiving information, helping someone to escape to England — anything but this.

'Simon,' Levenson had added while Leigh was still too stunned to speak, 'you must do nothing, absolutely nothing, to arouse their suspicions, either before or after. Simply because you are a foreigner and worse, a foreigner from an unfriendly power, you will be under strict observation. Remember nothing you do must in any way make them think that you are anything but a straightforward businessman. If you are arrested which is quite possible, act like an indignant Englishman. Remember they will have no proof and if you stick to your story, it cannot be disproved. Unless they brainwash you,

you will be of no propaganda value to them and successful brainwashing is a long complicated business. Of course, I can't give you a written guarantee but I think if you keep calm and obey my instructions to the letter, you should be all right.'

Leigh had felt less reassured than ever by this and it was Gorebain who had once again taken the floor.

'Remember, Simon, if you succeed you will be saving the lives of a large number of our agents in East Germany. At the moment they are unaware that their covers have been blown and consequently are as dangerous to us as they once were to the Communists. If you fail, the damage that will result from their being caught will be incalculable. Contary to general supposition no man, however brave, can withstand physical pain beyond a certain degree. The Communists are masters at the art of torture and the truth drugs which they now use in conjunction with physical torture are almost guaranteed of success. So as well as signing their death warrants, if you fail, the information which will be extracted from each agent will do this country and certain of its allies, the greatest harm which it would take years to recover from.'

When finally, Leigh had stood up to go, the brandy bottle which Levenson had opened was empty. Gorebain made no move to leave and Leigh shook hands formally with him.

'Have a good trip, old boy, and don't think too badly of me,' he said.

Leigh had looked closely at the man who had been his friend for so long then he had smiled slightly. 'You're a wonderful actor, Peter, whatever else you are.'

At the door Levenson put his podgy hand on Leigh's shoulder. 'Good luck, Simon, and thank you.'

Leigh had turned back from the lift door and had looked hard at Levenson. 'Why me, Harold, why did you pick me?'

Levenson's reply had been foreboding but frank and Leigh whose dislike for the man had in no way diminished, respected him for this.

'Simon, any form of spy or espionage work is dangerous. Apart from your natural ability and intelligence, you have been chosen primarily because of your visit to East Germany. You were also selected because in the event of your being killed, you have no family or dependants. We spoke earlier of a gamble — the stakes are your life to lose and the lives of our agents to win. If you can keep your own life and at the same time save the lives of these agents, so much the better. If I'm completely honest with you, I would say the odds are slightly in the Bank's favour. So you will have to play your hand with skill and cunning. Good luck again, and remember you are completely on your own. If anything goes wrong we don't know you.'

★　★　★

Leigh shivered involuntarily as he remembered Levenson's words. He looked at his travelling clock — 9.27 — he had arranged to meet Davos and his wife in the Hotel bar at 9.30. He splashed some

Onyx on his face and went downstairs.

Davos was a large well built man, his dark, oily hair greying at the temples. He too, was a self-made man but unlike Leigh who hated any sign of show or ostentation, Davos liked to proclaim his wealth. He wore a shiny mohair suit and on his little finger was the largest diamond ring Leigh had ever seen; on his shirt front was displayed none too discreetly, the monogram P.D.

His wife, Marie, in complete contrast to her extrovert spouse, was petite and elegant in a plain blue angora dress. Both spoke good English and Davos made up for the lack of taste in his dress with his genuine charm and sense of humour.

'I am very pleased to meet you, Mr Leigh. I hope your visit to Belgium will be profitable and worthwhile.'

'I hope so, too,' replied Leigh.

'Tonight though,' continued Davos, 'there must be no business talk. We have the next few days to — how do you say — fly at each others throats. This evening is for relaxing and enjoyment.

Leigh smiled, relieved to find that he

would not have to talk facts and figures at least until the morning when he would be more rested and alert.

Within half an hour Leigh was on christian name terms with Davos and his wife and by the time they left the hotel for dinner, Leigh was feeling less tense than at any time since leaving London. 'I'm glad,' he thought, 'that I accepted this invitation after all.'

Davos had chosen a small club for dinner on the other side of the city and on the drive there in his white Ford Mustang, he promised Leigh the best lobster he had ever eaten.

'Do you know Brussels well, Simon?' asked Marie.

'Quite well,' replied Leigh, 'but I have never stayed here long enough on any one visit to really get to know the city as opposed to just knowing it.'

'It's the same with me and London,' said Davos braking hard to avoid running over a drunken sailor lurching uncertainly across the road. He swore at the man and continued, 'When I'm in London I seem to commute between my hotel and the offices of the people with whom I have come to do business and I never have the chance to see the real London.'

'Well, we'll have to do something about that,' replied Leigh. 'Next time you come over, I'll give you and Marie a guided tour.'

'That would be very nice. Marie, she loves London especially those shops.' He smiled at his wife. 'I could not get her away from one street. All day she walked up and down, up and down. What was the name of that street, cherie?'

Marie smiled and turned to look at Leigh.

'Bond Street. It's true Simon, all day I walked up and down the street. There were so many beautiful things to buy that by the time I had made up my mind about a handbag and some porcelain dishes all the shops were closed.'

Leigh laughed. 'My wife was the same, she could never make up her mind what to buy.'

'You are going straight back to London when you leave Brussels?' Davos asked, not wanting to ask if Leigh was divorced or if his wife was dead.

'No. First I'm going to Germany.'

'Ah, I was in Hamburg last month. How that city has grown and prospered since the war. You know, Simon, economically through losing the war, Germany has come out on top. Millions of dollars and pounds have been poured into her by the so called victors and now Germany flourishes while Britain struggles on.'

Leigh agreed and added, 'I'm not going to Hamburg. I'm going to East Germany, East Berlin, in fact.'

'They want computers in East Germany?' Davos asked in surprise. 'From what one reads most people there hardly have enough money to buy food and clothes and yet they want to spend money on computers?'

'So it would appear,' replied Leigh. 'They are very interested in some Data Logging equipment we have recently developed.'

'I would not like to go to East Berlin,' said Marie. 'There's something about the place with its inhuman wall and soldiers that frightens me.'

Leigh did not want to spend the evening talking about East Berlin and he was relieved when the car pulled up in a narrow cobbled street which was brightly lit with old-fashioned gas lamps.

'Here we are, Simon. Come on Marie, let's show the British that the Belgians also know how to enjoy themselves.'

'I have no doubt of that,' smiled Leigh as he followed Davos and his wife down some steps into a building with a white door on which was painted in gold leaf 'La Dolce Notte'. The club consisted of one large room sub-divided into two sections, one of which housed the bar and the other the dance floor cum stage and restaurant. Although still early by night-club standards, there was hardly a free table, but when Davos gave his name to the waiter they were immediately shown to a reserved table at the front of the room next to the stage. Leigh was always suspicious of dark basement clubs where one cannot see what one is eating, but the Lobster Thermidor that they had all ordered was as good as he had ever tasted at Overtons or Pruniers.

With the lobster Davos insisted that they drink champagne as a prelude to what he hoped would be a successful trip for Leigh. Here again, the champagne, a vintage Bollinger, well iced and very dry was excellent, and a far cry from the usual 'FIZZ' served in most London clubs at £5 a bottle.

After the meal Davos and his wife drank brandy but Leigh stuck to Scotch.

'Was I boasting about the lobster?' asked Davos smiling proudly at Leigh.

'Not in the least, Paul. I enjoyed it very much indeed. Thank you.'

At midnight the cabaret was due to begin and at exactly 11.45 the lights dimmed and a drum roll began. Leigh was surprised that there was no introduction to the cabaret.

Davos leaned across the table and whispered in Leigh's ear, 'This you'll enjoy even more than the lobster.'

Leigh smiled and obediently he sat back waiting expectantly for what was to come. Generally he hated cabarets and looking around him, was surprised at the sudden silence and the air of excitement and anticipation which seemed to have gripped the audience.

When his eyes had grown more accustomed to the dark he again looked around the club. All attention was focused on the empty stage. The room was now completely without light except for the glow of cigarettes and cigars. The drum roll which had reached a climax stopped abruptly. Not a sound came from any of the tables. There was something inexplicably strange about the silence of more than a hundred people in a dark room. The feeling of excitement and expectancy in the audience was transmitted to Leigh; he took a long drink from his glass. Once again the drum roll began. This time more softly with a rhythmic sensuality which reminded Leigh of the sound of Tom-Toms he had once heard in South Africa. He had been staying in a small village lying next to a forest which stretched for hundreds of miles. The Tom-Toms which had started in the middle of the night and gone on for four hours had kept him awake. There was something haunting and strangely frightening about the sound which they emitted. The next morning Leigh had been told that the Tom-Toms during the night were a voodoo call: someone was about to die. He shuddered at the memory.

The drums stopped, again silence. Leigh could just make out Marie Davos' face from the glow of his cigar. Her eyes were unblinking and held a look of intensity and concentration.

Suddenly a white spotlight darted on to the stage, almost immediately it was turned off. The darkness of the room and the unnerving silence was interrupted by some footsteps. Leigh strained his eyes and with difficulty could make out the silhouette of a girl on the stage. Tall, with long hair, she wore a pale coloured evening gown which reached to the floor. She stood motionless on the stage, her head held high, her arms at her side. Again the spotlight came on and slowly focused on the girl's face. Before him stood one of the most beautiful girls Leigh had ever seen. Not a sound from the audience broke the spell which had fallen on the club. Every eye in the room, was riveted to the girl on the stage. She was not as tall as she had appeared in the total darkness, about 5′ 8″ Leigh guessed. Her skin was dark from the sun and on her face there was no make-up other than on her lips which were a flash of frosty pink. High cheekbones and wide set ice blue eyes were framed by long black hair. Her dress, which was white, was simple to the extreme with no frills or decoration; it was silk and around her waist was a wide, black leather belt with a gold clasp. She wore no jewellery other than a heavy gold chain around her neck with a star shaped emerald at the base where the bare skin below her neck met the top of her dress.

The silence which since the drums had ceased had been uninterrupted was replaced by a piano which began to play with feeling and great expression a Chopin concerto. It struck Leigh as odd that he was not at all surprised to find this sort of music being played here, in place of the usual night club medley of pop tunes.

The spotlight did not move from the girl's face, and with her eyes fixed on some indiscriminate point towards the back of the room she slowly raised her hands to her neck and unclasped the gold chain necklace, which she placed on the table by her side. This was the first time that she had moved since she had come on to the stage but there was no easing of tension in the club and the electric atmosphere which had taken hold of everyone watching intensified. The girl's eyes were unnaturally bright and as Leigh watched her face for any sign of emotion he noticed that as she breathed her nostrils flared slightly as if she, like her audience, was tense and on edge. She had what film producers spend a fortune and a lifetime trying to manufacture, an air of sensuality and aloofness coupled with an aura of complete femininity. To Leigh with alcohol coursing through his veins and his emotions heightened by the atmosphere of the club, she represented the quintessence of everything he desired physically in a woman.

As the piano concerto built up to a

crescendo the girl put her hands to the back of her neck and gracefully without affection or suggestion unhooked the silk fastening at the top of her dress; then with her hands back at her sides she arched her back, slightly at first and then more until the zip unaided by her hands began to run slowly down the back of the dress. When it reached her waist she pushed the dress off her shoulders so that the top fell to the floor. The bottom half, still supported by the belt, remained as it was.

Leigh tore his eyes from the stage and glanced at Davos. The man was sweating freely although it was not overwarm in the room. There was a sudden break in the piano playing. The girl undid the belt and placed it carefully on the table next to the chain necklace; in one movement she stepped out of the dress. At the same time the spotlight went out leaving the room once more in darkness. The piano playing resumed. A cry of frustration and deprivation rose from the throats of the audience, women as well as men.

A moment later the spotlight reappeared, and now the girl, the dress at her feet, was standing with her back to the audience wearing only her bra and pants. Her legs which had been concealed by the dress were long and firm and the tan of her body was relieved only by the white of her skin above and below the bra strap and at the base of her spine by her pants. Her hair hung freely and fell well below her shoulders. Slowly she pirouetted to face the audience. She stood motionless. Leigh took a deep breath amazed at the sheer beauty and perfection of her body. Putting her hands again behind her back she undid the clasp of the bra and let it fall to the floor. Her breasts were proud and firm, rising visibly under her deep breathing.

After a moment she put her hands on her waist and slowly removed her pants, again the spotlight was extinguished and this time the noise from the audience was a cry of animal fury. When the light reappeared, the piano had ceased and the drums had taken its place. The girl stood on the stage, pure in her nakedness, unashamed of the animal sexuality she transmitted. She turned once so that her back was again towards the audience moving slowly, gracefully like a ballet dancer executing a simple but important movement, then once again facing the audience she bowed once; not low like a performer to an audience but like a princess acknowledging the homage of her subjects. The light went out and the drums ceased. There was no clapping from the audience, no cheers, none of the applause that usually follows a striptease. It was as if a superb actress had given the most moving artistic performance and the audience were still too overwhelmed to react.

When the wall lights came on a few minutes later, the stage was empty except for the table. Conversation in the club gradually resumed but it was some moments before anyone at Leigh's table spoke. At last Davos took a handkerchief from his pocket to wipe the perspiration from his face.

'Well, Simon, have you ever seen anything like that before?'

'Never,' replied Leigh, truthfully. He was amazed that the girl throughout her act had not used one provocative gesture, not one suggestive word, yet purely through her body and personality had exercised a magnetic hold on her audience.

'You know, Simon,' Davos continued, 'she does this as an art, she has private money and has no need to work, but in the same way that an artist finds self-expression in his painting or a writer in his books, so this girl expresses herself through her beautiful body.'

'But why here?' asked Leigh. 'Why in this little club?'

'Have you ever,' replied the Belgian, 'seen a more respectful, a more dignified audience at any ballet or opera?'

Leigh shook his head. 'What is the girl's name?' he asked.

'Suki,' replied Maria Davos. 'Suki Laval. You will meet her in a minute, she is a good friend of mine and she knew we were coming tonight.'

Leigh took another pull from his glass, which was nearly empty. Since Klaire's death he had not touched another woman. He had had many opportunities but for stupid reasons some irrational even to himself, he had remained faithful to her memory. Perhaps the strongest reason was that he had never met a woman who matched up to Klaire, but in four long years he had not so much as kissed a woman. He knew that sooner or later he would have to break this self-imposed 'fast'.

Couples were dancing now and the atmosphere had almost returned to the normal nightclub atmosphere of laughter, noise and music. From a concealed door to the left of the stage walked the girl who fifteen minutes previously had held the audience enthralled by her performance. Every eye in the room was on her as she walked over to Marie Davos and kissed her on both cheeks. She had changed into a plain, black dress but around her neck was the same heavy chain that she had worn on stage. Her face was still without make-up except for the pink lips. Leigh who had stood up with Davos as she approached the table studied her trying to find a flaw close to that he might have missed while she was on the stage, but even now one of the many, amongst the rest of the women in the club, she epitomized to Leigh the ultimate in beauty and desire.

After Davos had kissed her, he said, 'Suki, I would like you to meet Simon Leigh, an English business colleague of mine, Simon, Suki Laval.'

Was it his imagination or had the girl frowned when Davos mentioned his name.

Suki Laval inclined her head and smiled very slightly as she took Leigh's outstretched hand. There was something about the girl which was familiar to Leigh and it annoyed him that he could not place what it was. When the waiter brought a chair for her to sit down it suddenly came to him. She was wearing the same scent that Klaire had always used — Jean Patou's 'Joy'. It was the only scent in the world that Leigh could have recognized and identified by name. The girl was speaking to him and he forced his mind back to what she was saying.

'I'm sorry, I was dreaming. What did you say?'

Again the half smile appeared on her face. 'I asked if you were in Brussels for long, Mr Leigh?'

Leigh was struck by the fluency and lack of accent in her English. 'Just five days,' he replied.

'Five days, and five nights,' Davos interrupted laughing.

Leigh smiled. 'If we're going to be that precise it's five days and four nights.'

Leigh insisted on ordering the next round of drinks.

'What would you like, Mademoiselle Laval?' Leigh asked.

'My name is Suki, and I would like Vodka.'

'Neat?' asked Leigh.

'Neat, and please ask the waiter for the Russian or Polish Vodka. Vodka which is distilled in Western Europe has a completely different taste.'

Leigh smiled and complied with her request. 'Not just a beautiful face,' he thought. 'Here is a girl who knows her own mind.'

5

Getting to Know You

As far as Suki was concerned her act was far more than a striptease. It was as Davos had explained to Leigh 'her way of expressing herself, her art'. She was extremely sensitive to her audience and knew instinctively that she had been good tonight.

Before she had been introduced to the dark Englishman with the strangely attractive green eyes, she had made up her mind to have one quick drink with Paul and Marie Davos and go straight home to bed. It was surprising how tiring half an hour on that stage was.

She had frowned when Davos had introduced her to Simon Leigh because she had been taken by surprise and was unprepared. The orders which she had received that morning from the General had stipulated that she was to make contact with him. How and when was her problem. But here he was sitting next to her as large as life. It could not be a coincidence of names. She knew that Davos was in the electronics business and the very brief information the General had given her had mentioned that Leigh's Company manufactured computers. No, this was the Simon Leigh of whom the General had written in his precise handwriting at the bottom of her typed instructions, 'Get to know this man. Gain his confidence by *any* means. You have five days to find out all there is to know about him.'

After the initial shock, Suki had almost immediately recovered her customary composure, but she knew the frown of surprise must have shown on her face if only for a second when Leigh's name was mentioned.

'Had Simon Leigh noticed the frown?' To look at he was no fool but even if he had seen it he could not have known the reason for it — that is if he was the innocent businessman he professed to be.

Leigh asked Suki if she had eaten. She

said she had not but was not hungry. Leigh guessed that it would take some time for this girl to unwind. Perhaps she was like him and lived off nervous energy and the occasional rare steak.

'Whereabouts in England to you come from?' asked Suki suddenly.

'I live in London,' Leigh replied. 'Do you know it?'

'A little,' said the girl. 'I was educated at a convent in Brighton.'

'That explains your fluent English.' Leigh smiled. 'You are Belgian?'

'No. My father was French, my mother is Hungarian, but I have made my home here in Brussels for the past few years.'

Leigh tried to ask her about herself but she seemed reluctant to talk, preferring to question him. 'Are you in Brussels to do business with Paul?'

'I hope so,' said Leigh.

For a while Suki and Marie Davos talked and suddenly some remark from Marie made Suki's face, which Leigh was studying, light up in a smile. This was the first time she had really smiled and Leigh had been thinking that she had a sad expression in her eyes, as if she had known much unhappiness. When she smiled, Leigh noticed that her two front teeth were not quite even and he found this slight imperfection very appealing — it was comforting to know that this nightclub 'goddess' was human after all. He noticed that she kept clasping and unclasping her hands as if nervous and upset about something. Her fingers were long and her nails short and unpolished.

Paul and Marie stood up to dance and Leigh moved his chair so he was opposite her and could look at her openly. She returned his gaze, her eyes proud and challenging. Leigh could now see that her eyes were more grey than blue. They really were very sad eyes. Leigh wanted to kiss them and make them laugh.

Instead he said, 'Have you worked here long?'

'About six months. I like it here — I am treated as an artist and not as an animal on public display.'

When Davos returned with Marie from the dance floor he rubbed his eyes theatrically in mock tiredness.

'I can't keep up with you night people, Simon. When you get to my age you have to begin to take life easy otherwise you end up with ulcers or cirrhosis of the liver. Come on Marie, let's go home and leave the children to play.'

Everyone laughed. Davos who was no more than forty, had the energy of an eighteen-year-old and was usually the last person to leave any party or nightclub. While Marie and Suki were saying their goodbyes, Davos and Leigh made their plans for the following day. It was arranged that a car would be sent to Leigh's hotel at nine o'clock to bring him to Davos' office.

Leigh thanked Davos for a wonderful evening and after another round of goodbye hand-shakes the couple left the club hand in hand.

It had been a long time since Leigh had been really excited by a woman, not just physically, but excited by her as a person. For four years his time had been taken up almost completely by his business, with gambling providing the only form of recreation. This he now kept to a once or twice a month visit to Crockfords or the 21 Club where he played heavily often winning, but since the 'reckless period' just after Klaire's death when he had gone a little mad, he never now lost more than he could afford. As he sat looking at the beautiful girl with the proud face beside him, he felt an inexplicable sensation of excitement and danger.

Later Leigh could not recall what they had talked about. He remembered standing up to dance with Suki. The 'pocket-handkerchief' dance floor was very crowded and Leigh had no idea what time it was. He was fascinated by this strange girl with the sad eyes. 'Was she really as self-sufficient and independent as she seemed or underneath her beauty and self-confidence was she insecure and frightened?' Also it was not right for a girl with such talent and beauty to have so much sadness in her face. What had happened to her to make her so unhappy — a tragic love affair? The death of a loved one?

'Or perhaps I'm dreaming,' thought

Leigh. 'And she is a perfectly normal well-balanced girl who seems sad to me because I'm a bit drunk and would like her to be sad so that she will cry on my shoulder, and I can play Sir Galahad and help her with whatever it is that is troubling her.'

Suki was annoyed with herself. She was far more affected by Simon Leigh than she had any right or wish to be. She kept telling herself that this was just another job. Simon Leigh, just another subject on whom she had to file a report. But job or no job she was a human being and she felt that she held an unfair advantage or was it a disadvantage in that she already knew considerably more about Leigh than he did about her. She would be denied the 'getting to know you' process which she found the most exciting and stimulating part of a relationship. Mentally she kicked herself. Relationship! There was no relationship. It was a job, just a job. Anyway all things considered, she did not know such an awful lot about Simon Leigh. It was because so little was known that the

General had instructed her to find out more. She tried to recall the General's brief dossier which was basically information gleaned from Leigh's Visa Application Form and passport.

Name:	Simon Leigh.
Age:	34.
Height:	5′ 11″
Hair:	Dark brown.
Eyes:	Green.
Weight:	174 lbs.
Occupation:	Self-employed business-man manufacturing computers and business machines.
Marital status:	Widower.

That was all the information the General had given her. The photograph which was clipped to the report had not done justice to Leigh. Suki thought it made him look cruel and ruthless.

There was a separate dossier under four major headings to be returned to the General duly completed.

Characteristics
Interests
Weaknesses
Comments

Suki knew that one of these dossiers properly compiled could give a complete stranger an intimate knowledge of any given man or woman.

Leigh was saying something to her. She forgot the General and dossiers and the job she had to do.

'My wife used to wear that scent. It is Joy, isn't it?'

'Yes,' she said. 'It is Joy. You are married, Simon?'

'Not anymore. My wife was killed in a car crash four years ago.'

'I am sorry.' How inadequate those three words were, she thought, and yet what else could one say. 'Did you love her very much?'

'Yes.'

They moved closer to each other on the dance floor, her cheek was soft against his. He stroked her long, soft hair. He kissed her forehead and her nose. She lifted her mouth to Leigh's and they kissed, slowly at first and then fiercely like old lovers. Leigh felt intoxicated by this girl and for the first time in four years he felt alive, carefree, even happy. When the band stopped playing, she began to move away. Their eyes met and she came back into his arms, They danced for a long time, both happy, both very much aware of each other. While the band was changing the music Leigh looked at his watch — 3.30.

'Let's sit down and have a drink after the next dance,' he said.

Suki nodded and smiled. The music started again but they did not start dancing for some moments, so engrossed were they in looking at each other. When the music stopped, Leigh kissed the girl on her cheek and led her back to their table.

'That was a very paternal kiss,' she said lightly, when they were seated at their table.

'A foretaste of things to come,' Leigh replied and again Suki gave her half smile.

Leigh was sick of drinking Scotch. He guessed he must have already consumed about three-quarters of a bottle since leaving his hotel. He had an acid taste in his mouth. He called the waiter.

'Bring two large vodkas, neat.' As the waiter departed, he called after him. 'Make it a bottle. We can help ourselves.'

'Do you always drink as much as this?' Suki asked, with genuine concern.

'Not always,' he replied. He took a cigar from his case and at once his new found happiness evaporated. Levenson, Gorebain, East Germany, never far from his thoughts, came flooding to the forefront of his mind. The match with which he was lighting his cigar flickered and went out, so much was his hand shaking.

Suki held his hand tightly and looked at him curiously. 'What's the matter, Simon?' she asked. 'You have gone deathly pale.'

'No, I am fine,' he said. 'It must be the heat.' At that moment the bottle of Polish Vodka arrived in answer to Leigh's silent prayer.

Before long the Vodka bottle was half empty and as they drank and talked and laughed, Leigh knew as he had known with Klaire, that human happiness can only be brought about with love and affection between two people. He was surprised by the number of questions Suki asked him about himself, but it flattered his ego to have someone so interested in him and he answered all her questions willingly.

When the Vodka bottle had diminished yet further, they decided to leave the club. Leigh called for the bill but the waiter told him that Monsieur Davos had left instructions that 'l'addition' was to be charged to him and nothing Leigh could say would induce the man to give him the bill. He gave the waiter a large tip and waited while Suki fetched her coat.

Dawn was breaking over Brussels as they emerged from the club into the narrow cobbled street. The sun, low on the horizon was a soft orange orb set in a dramatically fiery red sky.

They walked for some time silent and close before finding a taxi.

The discreet night porter at the Palace Hotel nodded gravely to Simon and Suki as they walked across the close carpeted foyer towards the lift. The liftman who had seen enough scandal in his twenty years in the hotel to shock a call-girl, thought they made a nice couple. The tall, quietly dressed Englishman and the beautiful girl with the long black hair.

When they were in Leigh's room they stood face to face, exploring one another's faces, each trying to read the other's mind.

'You know,' said Suki, 'every night men ask me to sleep with them, but surprise you as it may, I refuse. I think it is immoral to make love with someone whom you do not like, let alone love. I do not know you very well, Simon, and I have not known you very long, but I know I like you.' She said this with sincerity because it was true. 'I think it is equally immoral not to make love to someone you like regardless of how long you have known him.'

Leigh did not know what to reply. He sat down on the bed and gestured for the girl to come and sit next to him.

'Suki,' he said quietly taking the girl's face in his hands, and looking into the depths of her sad grey eyes. 'I have not been to bed with a girl since my wife died. It is stupid I know, but I always promised myself that when I did, it would also be with someone I liked a lot. In my case it has nothing to do with morals. It is selfish really, I suppose. It is just that before tonight, I have never really come across anyone I wanted badly enough.'

The girl's eyes were moist. 'I will try not to disappoint you, *chéri*,' she said, and kissed him again on the cheek.

For the second time that night, Suki undressed and when she was wearing only her bra and pants she turned to Leigh and lifted her arms for him to undo her brassiere. Then she stepped out of her pants and stood naked before him.

She would not let Leigh undress himself. 'In Japan,' she said, 'the man is the absolute master. He does not have to lift a finger. The girl takes pleasure in being his slave and obeying his every wish. I do not know that I altogether agree with the philosophy, but I think the basis is right. Women in the West want to be equal to men on the one hand, and on the other they expect to have doors opened for them by men. To be taken out to dinner by men, to be supported by men, where is the logic in that?'

Leigh laughed at her serious face and kissed her breasts, which became firm and pointed with desire.

★　★　★

It seemed only a few minutes after they had gone to bed, that Leigh's 7.30 alarm call came through from the reception desk. Although he had had less than three hours sleep, after a cold shower and two cups of hot, black coffee he felt refreshed and relaxed. Suki wanted to get out of bed too, but he made her stay.

'It's silly for both of us not to get enough sleep. Stay where you are and go back to sleep.'

When he was dressed he leant over the bed and kissed her. She had put on his blue pyjamas which were too big for her.

91

She looked both desirable and vulnerable. He wished he could have stayed and made love to her again. It had been good for both of them.

'It is said,' said Leigh, 'that the true test of a woman's beauty is how she looks first thing in the morning. You have just passed that test with flying colours.'

Suki looked away and the sad expression which had temporarily left her face, returned. 'Beauty,' she said quietly, 'is what you are like inside. Not your outward appearance.'

'That's a very profound remark for this time of the morning,' smiled Leigh.

She reached up and dragged him down to the bed, beside her.

'No darling,' he protested. 'I've got to go. Later.'

They fought playfully until at last Leigh managed to tear himself away. He kissed her sad eyes, still full of sleep.

At the door he turned. 'Have dinner with me tonight, before your performance?'

She nodded.

'See you back here later. I don't know

what time it will be but order anything you want from Room Service.' He blew her a kiss and left the room.

He went down to the foyer. It was ten to nine. He would have to forgo breakfast. He decided he was not hungry anyway.

Davos' driver was waiting and led him out to a gleaming black Citroen D.S.

Later in the morning after coffee and a bath, Suki put on the same dress she had taken off last night and smiled at herself in the mirror. 'Sinful child,' she mouthed at her reflection.

She left the hotel and returned to her small, exquisitely furnished apartment less than two kilometres away. She changed into flared camel trousers and a black cashmere poloneck.

Then remembering what she had been trying to forget, she picked up the telephone and sent a cable to the General. It was short and to the point.

'CONTACT MADE STOP WILL PROCEED AS ORDERED.'

On the dressing-table in her bedroom was a faded photograph of a woman of about sixty standing outside a café with a cheerful striped awning. The woman was very plain with dull grey hair, severely tied in a bun, framing her tired, pale face. The only outstanding feature about her was her eyes, which even in the dull black and white photograph stood out clear and bright like Suki's. Suki kissed the photograph and put it down.

She lay down on her bed and closed her eyes tightly. 'I must not get involved with Simon Leigh. I must remain detached and at the same time give him the impression of being fond of him. This is a job, just a job. Simon Leigh is an ordinary man. There is nothing special about him.' But it was no good. However many times she kept repeating this to herself she knew it was too late. She could not master or conquer her feelings for him. At last she slept.

When Leigh returned to the hotel at 6.30 there was no sign of Suki, and the Receptionist said there were no messages for him. He had had a good day with Davos and after hours of tough bargaining they had agreed price structures and delivery dates. Tomorrow the order should be signed which left Leigh three clear days in Brussels to see the other two companies with whom he had come to do business.

After a quick shower Leigh put on his bathrobe and pouring out a stiff whisky lay down on the bed. Two nights with little or no sleep was beginning to tell. He was disappointed that Suki was not here to greet him, but he reasoned that she had probably returned to her flat to change. It struck him as ridiculous that he did not even know where she lived.

As he was refilling his glass, the telephone rang. He picked up the receiver on the second ring.

'Hello, *chéri*, it's Suki.'

'Hello, sweetie, where are you?' Leigh asked.

'I'm in my apartment. I've been thinking; it's crazy for you to stay in the hotel. Why not move in here with me? I've everything you want and I offer a very high class of room service!'

Leigh laughed. She was right, it would be much better from all points of view.

'O.K. darling, give me your address and

telephone number for me to leave here with the hotel in case my London office ring.'

This done, Suki said, 'Simon, I'm cooking dinner here for you tonight. It will be good and very special.'

'That's wonderful. I look forward to it. I'll be with you in about an hour.'

'Au revoir, *chéri*.'

Leigh could not wait to see Suki again. He picked up the telephone. 'Can you get my bill ready, please. I'm afraid I have to leave suddenly.'

'There is nothing wrong, I hope, Monsieur?' asked the receptionist, who had listened in to Leigh's conversation with Suki.

'No, nothing at all.'

'I see, Monsieur. Yes certainly. It will be ready in ten minutes.' The girl winked at the other receptionist who giggled, she too had listened in to Leigh's phone-call.

6

Live for the Moment

London unpredictably was warm and sunny. Couples walked happily in the parks. Winter overcoats were finally shed — for how long no one knew.

'London is a very surprising city,' thought Gorebain, 'that's what makes it so appealing.' He was walking through St James' Park with the P.P.S. to the Foreign Secretary.

'So you don't anticipate any trouble with this latest recruit of yours, Gorebain?' asked the man blown up with good food and self-importance.

'No, sir, I don't. Everything should go according to plan. I have known this man Leigh for fifteen years and he is One hundred per cent reliable.'

'He didn't object to the mission?'

'I won't say he was over enthusiastic, sir, but he agreed and he won't let us down. I would stake my job on it.'

'You may have to,' thought the P.P.S. to himself, trying hard to keep his eyes from the pair of long legs beneath the short skirt, pushing the pram in front of them.

'One final word,' said the P.P.S. as the two men stood at the park gates before going their separate ways. 'The Minister asked me to tell you that he really is very concerned that everything goes well this time. To quote his exact words,' said the man puffing himself up, 'there is always a reason for failure but seldom a justification.'

Gorebain took a taxi back to the Admiralty and went straight to his small office on the fourth floor.

'Get Mr Levenson on the phone, please,' he said to his plump bespectacled secretary.

He sat at his desk and smoked two cigarettes before Levenson came on the line.

'Harold,' he said. 'The Minister is putting the pressure on. I don't like it.'

'Don't worry, Peter,' said Levenson. 'If we fail on this job his neck's just as much for the chop as anyone else's. That's what's really bothering him.'

Feeling less reassured than ever Gorebain replaced the receiver and returned to his routine paper work.

★ ★ ★

The next few days passed quickly for Leigh. He could not remember having been so happy for a long time. During his negotiations with the Belgians he forgot what he had to do in East Berlin, but suddenly for no reason he would remember and begin to sweat. It was like going to sleep on a difficult problem; one is always surprised to find that it is still there on waking in the morning.

The Belgians were very tight on price and they wanted special credit facilities but they wanted to buy and were prepared to place substantial orders. Leigh was concerned that he would not be able to meet the required delivery dates on his present output, but there was nothing he could do about that until he returned to London. 'If I ever do return,' he thought grimly to himself.

He phoned his office every day; everything seemed to be running smoothly there. 'I will make Joyce a Director at Christmas,' Leigh decided. The man had been with him since the beginning and apart from his unswerving loyalty he had done things for Leigh far outside his line of duty as Factory Manager. Leigh preferred to run his business as essentially a one man show but he knew better than most that no one was indispensable. The time had arrived when he must start to delegate responsibility.

It was wonderful to know each day that he had Suki to go back to in the evenings. He had forgotten what it was like to be pampered, asked about his day, his business, himself.

The first night when he had moved into Suki's apartment, after an excellent dinner of coq au vin followed by fresh peaches in Kirsch, Suki had telephoned La Dolce Notte and told them that she had a migraine and would not be in that night. Even though it was such short notice they had not tried to make her come.

'They need me far more than I need them.' She had smiled at Leigh as she replaced the receiver.

Apart from the wine at dinner they had drunk a lot of whisky between them and then talked for many hours. Still Suki did not talk much about herself, but from the little she did say, Leigh learned that her French father had emigrated to Hungary before the war and had opened a restaurant there which he had run with his wife until he died.

'So your mother is still in Hungary?' asked Leigh.

'Yes,' said Suki, her eyes sadder than ever. 'She is still there.'

The girl picked up the photograph of the old lady under the striped awning, which she had been looking at earlier in the day.

Leigh took it and looked closely, recognizing in the old lady, the same clear eyes as Suki had. 'She looks a fine person,' said Leigh.

'She is a fine person,' said Suki and changed the subject.

Around midnight she had poured the

last drop of Scotch into Leigh's cut glass tumbler. When he protested she told him she had another bottle, which she fetched from the kitchen. She undid the bottle and came and sat at his feet on a brocade footstool.

Reaching out, she took hold of his hand and looked far into his eyes as if searching for something. Leigh wanted to make her smile and laugh; for such a wonderful person to have such a tragic face was wrong. Whatever sorrow she had known and Leigh was now convinced that he had not been mistaken about her unhappiness, he wanted to make her happy again. He had met the girl less than twenty-four hours earlier, but felt as if he had known her for years.

Once or twice that night, Leigh had considered telling her about what he had to do in East Germany, but he realized that this would be a dangerous and extremely stupid gesture which could cause great harm to a lot of people. Also, however much of a burden it was to carry around in his mind, it would be grossly unfair to share it with Suki who obviously had her own troubles in full measure.

Before they had gone to bed Suki had made coffee which she laced generously with whisky. As she came out of the small kitchen carrying the tray she looked at Leigh, who smiled at her. 'For the first time in my life,' she thought, as she put the tray down on the table in front of him, 'I have fallen in love with a man. And I have to betray him: Judas the second, except he did it for money.'

She sat once again at his feet. 'Simon,' she said, 'I want you to know that whatever happens, I love you.'

'What do you mean, whatever happens?' he asked.

'Nothing,' she said quietly. 'Let's talk about something else.'

★　★　★

On Leigh's last night in Belgium they drove in Suki's little Renault Dauphine to a Chateau just outside Brussels which had been converted into a restaurant. The whole atmosphere of the place was reminiscent of the pre-war capitals of

Europe with the men immaculate in dinner clothes and the women elegant and chic in long dresses. The whole chateau was lit only by candlelight and the décor was refreshingly simple and uncluttered.

'It is good to see you enjoying yourself, *chéri*,' said Suki suddenly, as they danced and clapped and sang uninhibitedly along with all the other patrons of the restaurant who were reacting to the excellent band. Leigh stopped his uncharacteristic frivolity and looked at Suki. She was right. He was enjoying himself immensely. Whether he was trying that much harder because of his impending trip to East Germany, now only hours away, or whether it was merely the effect of Suki's stimulating company, he did not know but he had not been so happy for a long time; if only there was not this enormous raincloud on the horizon.

'I'm glad you know how to appreciate life, *chéri*,' said Suki as they sipped their drinks and watched the others dancing for a change. 'Most Englishmen are too shy and introvert to ever let themselves really go.'

'It's the whisky,' smiled Leigh. 'I never usually unwind as much as this.'

There had been a time not so long ago when Simon Leigh had not appreciated life at all. He thought back to Klaire's funeral, still as clear in his mind as if it had been yesterday. After the service the Priest who was about the same age as Leigh, had taken his arm and walked him, still stunned and unwilling to believe that she had really gone, from the new grave back to his car.

'Simon,' the Priest had said, 'the pain will be lasting and deep and this is only right, but one day you will have to come to life again.'

At the time Leigh had not believed this possible but gradually although he would never completely get over Klaire's death, he had pulled himself together, working eighteen hours a day to forget. Now, after four long years, it seemed he was coming to life again.

'Simon,' said Suki a little later when the tempo of the music had quietened to the unashamedly romantic strains of Charles Chaplin's 'Limelight'. 'What will happen when you go to East Germany. I mean what will happen to us?'

Leigh, who had been putting off this thought, looked across at the beautiful girl beside him. As always, she was wearing the heavy gold chain around her neck which she had worn the first night he had seen her.

'I'll try and stop off at Brussels on my way back, but anyway you must come to London very soon.'

'That would be wonderful,' she said. 'Where would we go?'

'Wherever you like, darling.'

'In that case,' she said smiling, 'Ascot, The Savoy, Annabels and all the in places.'

Leigh laughed. 'Not all at once, I hope. I had better do some profitable business here to pay for all this good-living.'

'When I left my Convent,' said Suki, 'and was in London for a while before returning to Hungary, I was too young to go anywhere exciting but now . . .'

'Now,' interrupted Leigh, 'you are a big

girl and you shall go everywhere.'

He called for the bill. 'Let's go home. It's all very well for you women of leisure to go gallivanting all night long, but us working men have to be up early.'

Laughing they left the chateau.

When they were back in Suki's apartment, Leigh who felt very tired went straight to bed. As he lay there waiting for Suki, it began to rain. The rhythm of the raindrops assailing the window pane was strangely soothing and peaceful. At last Suki came in from the sitting-room where she said she had some writing to do.

'Suki,' Simon asked as he watched her undressing. 'How long are you going to go on working in that Club?'

'Until I find something more permanent,' she replied. The girl looked straight ahead and then she came and sat on the bed and kissed him. Suddenly for no apparent reason she began to cry, soundlessly at first like a small child and then her body began to shake, giving way to an uncontrollable sobbing. She raised her head and looked at Leigh and through her tears he could see that her eyes, always sad, were filled now with fear. He pulled her face down on to his shoulder where her sobbing diminished into a pitiful whimpering. She put her arms around his neck and buried her face in his shoulder.

'What is the matter, darling, what's the matter. Tell me. I can't help you if you won't tell me what's wrong.'

'I can't,' she sobbed. 'Oh, Simon, I'm so alone, so afraid. I love you. I really love you.'

'I love you too, Suki,' he said and meant it.

She ceased sobbing for a moment and looked at him, her eyes almost happy. 'You do, Simon, you promise me you do?'

'I promise you, Suki.'

'Whatever happens?' she asked.

'Whatever happens,' he said, not understanding but not wanting to cause her more pain by questioning her about something which she obviously did not want to talk. He began to stroke her hair slowly like a father comforting his daughter after a nightmare and her sobbing which she had began to control became worse and her whole body shook in his arms.

'It's all right, darling, it's all right. I will take care of you.' He knew that when she was ready she would tell him what it was that was making her so terribly unhappy. Meanwhile, he would not probe anymore. He would provide the shoulder she so badly needed to cry on. Soon her sobbing stopped and she kissed him tenderly at first and then passionately.

'*Chéri*,' she said, her voice choked with recent tears, 'make love to me, please. I want you so much.'

Leigh undressed her while she lay still on the bed. He kissed every part of her body and made love to her with a passion of which he had not known himself capable.

★   ★   ★

The General was terminating a lecture to students at the Central College of Defence (Spy Training School). His lecture that day had been concerned with the passing and receiving of information.

'Tomorrow, Gentlemen,' he said, 'I will give you a practical demonstration of the microdot. The principle of the microdot is that an entire document can be reduced to the size of a punctuation mark innocently appearing in a letter. To give you an idea of the effectiveness of the microdot, it has been said that all the hundreds of thousands of books in the Library of Culture could by this method be stored in ten filing cabinets.

'With this thought, Gentlemen, I leave you until tomorrow.'

The General collected his papers and left. Once more in his office he smoked a cigarette as he did whenever concentrating and opened the report which had just been placed on his desk. A smile of satisfaction crossed his smooth aristocratic face as he read it, absorbing every word. He was a great believer in these reports which he had initiated and believed they were far more efficient than any other method currently employed by the Soviet or Allied Intelligence Networks.

'What an asset women are,' he thought,

'if properly utilized.' He settled back and read the folder for the second time, this time building up a mental picture of the man depicted in the report, which would be impregnably imprinted on his brain.

Name   Simon Leigh
Report   Class A. 100 Personal
Agent   49003 (Brussels XRP)

GENERAL CHARACTERISTICS

Subject is a man of habit and routine. He employs moderation in all things with the possible exception of drinking. On several occasions I observed him consume considerable amounts of alcohol but at no time did he lose his self-control or show any outward signs of intoxication.

He smokes only cigars, always Dutch during the day and in the evening Havana.

Subject enjoys good food but eats only one main meal a day (evening). He dresses well in an English way. His suits are all hand tailored (Label Harlington and Swann, 10 Sackville Street) and are all in plain colours of wool composition. The jackets are cut long with one centre vent. Suits all two piece. His shirts (Label Coles) mostly pale blue and white (all have cuff-link fastening). Ties all silk, all plain colours. Shoes all black, all laceless, some elasticated boots, some slip-on casuals.

Subject never wears a hat and has a white raincoat and camelhair overcoat.

General Information
Subject shaves with a hand razor (heavy Gillette). Wears no ring or jewellery of any kind. Uses Onyx Aftershave and Christian Dior Cologne. Uses no hair dressing. Subject only uses showers, claims 'baths unhygienic as dirt stays in water'.

('There is truth in that,' thought the General, enjoying the mental picture being built up of the man.)

Interests
His business.
Gambling.

Hobbies
Subject plays squash once a week and has an interest in sailing.

Weaknesses
Gambling possibly — I have not seen the subject gamble. I do not know how strongly this vice affects him. He has told me he finds it very relaxing, quote 'one exchanges one set of worries (business worries, presumably) for another.'

General Comments
Wife killed in a car crash four years ago. Subject very much affected by her death, although he does not show it. Superficially very unemotional and undemonstrative. Highly intelligent. Has high principles. Too easy going in some ways. Sexually proficient. (The General chuckled as he read this and lit another cigarette.) A thorough search of his personal effects failed to reveal anything of a suspicious nature which could conceivably be utilized for espionage work.

Conclusion
Subject is a bona fide businessman.

The rest of the report contained a detailed account of the time Suki had spent with Leigh. Where they had been. What Leigh had said. Here also the conclusion was the same.

The General put down the report, pleased with himself. He asked his Secretary to have Donecke come in. When the little man came bustling in, his face the epitome of hardship and struggle, there were two glasses of Remy Martin Black Market brandy on the General's desk.

'Ah, Hans. I have just had the report on Leigh. You have nothing to worry about except doing good business with him. The man is in the clear. We cannot be too careful though,' he added as if in defence of all the trouble he had been to. 'Remember Greville Wynne.'

Donecke who did not particularly like brandy drank the health of Comrade Kosygin, Comrade Ulbricht and the Party.

'He smokes Havanas, you know,' said the General. 'Perhaps he will give me a box as a souvenir of his visit to our fair city.'

Donecke, who thought the General's extravagances were shameful and corrupt, drank to this too.

★   ★   ★

On the morning of his departure from Brussels, Suki drove Leigh out to the airport. On the short drive they did not speak much. When the small car drew up outside the Terminal building Leigh kissed Suki on the cheek as he made to get out of the car but she pulled him back and clung to him like a little child, her arms tight around his neck as if frightened to let go.

After a little while, Suki relaxed her grip on Leigh and kissed him once. 'Go, darling,' she said.

As he was walking away from the car, he stopped and turned to wave at Suki who was still sitting watching him. He could see that there were tears in her eyes. Suddenly she revved the engine fiercely and shot off without looking back.

Whilst waiting for his flight to be called, Leigh went to the Airport bar for a drink. 'Dutch courage,' he thought as he ordered a second.

'Will passengers on Aeroflot Flight 499 to East Berlin please check in at Customs Gate 7.' The message was repeated in French, German and Russian.

Leigh paid for his drinks and reluctantly left the comforting sanctuary of the bar.

'Have a good flight, sir,' the barman called after him in American accented English.

7

Romeo Y Julieta

The Ilyushin jet landed at Schonefeld Airport in blinding rain. As Leigh looked around his fellow passengers preparing to disembark from the aircraft, it seemed as if few of them were overjoyed to be there. There were not the usual smiles and laughter of men returning home to their families after a trip abroad; instead there was an atmosphere of grim acceptance and resignation. Most of them were East German scientists returning from a series of meetings in Brussels and Paris. After their brief taste of Capitalist delights it was no wonder that they were not happy to be returning to the austere, uneasy atmosphere of East Berlin, mused Leigh gathering together the papers he had been studying on the flight. The stewardess, however, smiled warmly at him as he walked down the steps of the plane on to

117

the wet shiny tarmac.

'Have a pleasant stay,' she called after him. He turned and smiled at her.

A Government representative was at the airport to meet him. He introduced himself as Hans Donecke from the Ministry of Trade. He shook hands with Leigh and clicked his heels.

After customs had been cleared with a minimum of formality he led Leigh out to a Wartburg painted an optimistic red. Leigh noticed that nearly every other car in sight was black. The uniformed chauffeur did not acknowledge either Leigh or Donecke. When the two men were installed in the back of the car which had black tinted windows Donecke turned to Leigh. He spoke good English, but with a guttural German accent.

'Herr Leigh, we have had you booked into the Hotel Mannheim. It is a very good hotel and I trust you will have a pleasant stay in the Federal Republic of East Germany.'

'A much rehearsed little speech,' thought Leigh, thanking the man for his trouble. As they drove along, Leigh surveyed the grey, drab buildings and half finished apartment blocks in evidence throughout the city. He mentally compared this communist half of Berlin according to propaganda, prosperous and thriving with its West German counterpart.

'No wonder they had to build a wall to stop people trying to escape to a better world.'

'There is to be a small dinner in your honour tomorrow evening. Herr Leigh,' said Donecke, interrupting Leigh's reverie. 'The launching we hope of a successful and profitable business relationship between us. The head of my department is giving the dinner.'

Leigh was badly shaken by this information, but he showed no surprise and smiled politely at Donecke. Levenson had said that it was inevitable that Leigh would come into contact with the General: as the head of the Government department which had invited Leigh to East Berlin, the whole success of his mission depended on it. But so soon, so openly, in the presence of God knows how many others. Leigh had been subconsciously preparing for this moment since leaving England, but somehow this was an anticlimax to all the fear and tension he had suffered. Tomorrow, no doubt, the fear and tension would return in full strength.

★ ★ ★

The hotel proved to be an imposing if somewhat dirty building which for some reason reminded Leigh of a Town Hall he had once seen somewhere. Inside it was very bright with strip fluorescent tubes traversing the high ceiling. The uncarpeted floor was laid with poor imitation parquet.

Herr Donecke was obviously a well-known figure in the hotel, as all the staff bowed obsequiously as Leigh followed the little German over to the formica topped reception desk. Here a plump, bald man, making a vain attempt to look smart in a pair of faded striped trousers and shabby black jacket also wished Herr Leigh a pleasant stay in the Federal Republic.

Leigh was pleasantly surprised to find that despite the hotel's outward appearance, his room was comfortable and modern and the adjoining bathroom had a shower as well as bath. Before unpacking, Leigh undressed and showered. He noticed a long, red mark running down his chest. 'Suki's mark,' he thought, smiling to himself and remembering with pleasure the nights he had spent with her.

He lay down on the bed and closed his eyes. It was essential that from now until he left East Berlin that he behaved absolutely naturally and did nothing to arouse the suspicions of his hosts. The time for fear and self-doubt was over. He was committed to do this job and however repulsive it was to him, he was going to do it as thoroughly and efficiently as possible.

During the war,[1] Leigh had always liked to mentally plan in advance his course of action as much as possible. It

[1] Korea.

was surprising how much more competently one operated when one had thought out every angle and he applied this process to his impending mission.

He cast his mind back to all he had learnt from Levenson about the Communist Espionage network. The extent of the man's knowledge had astonished Leigh, but as the head of M.I.6 the British Secret Service, with agents reporting to him from all over the world, he had to know his stuff. A newspaper had once described his position without mentioning his name, which they did not know, as 'one of the most powerful but least known men in England'. His business cover was effective and genuine.

'Simon,' he had said in his dry, cultured voice, 'as well as being the head of the spy network in East Germany the General is responsible for the infiltration and ultimate success of all Agents leaving East Germany on missions to Europe and the United States. The East Germans have had to operate closely with the K.G.B., the Russian equivalent of the American Central Intelligence Agency. As

East Germany is not officially recognized in most countries, they have to work rather more closely with the Russians than they would like. Very basically the K.G.B. operates overseas, mainly through an extensive network of Agents placed in its Embassies, missions and Official Agencies. The K.G.B. Officer in the Communist Embassy abroad may be the press attaché, the first Secretary or even conceivably the Ambassador himself; he may just as easily be a chauffeur or chef. Because these agents enjoy diplomatic immunity they cannot be arrested or imprisoned. At any hint of suspicion they are quietly recalled to Moscow or East Berlin and after a suitable lapse of time are despatched to some other country to continue their good work.

'As a man,' Levenson had continued, 'the General, apart from his over-indulgence and sadism is thoroughly evil. He has over a period of years, compiled a list of known British Agents operating in East Germany. When the moment is ripe, he will swoop and bring them all in. I promise you this, Simon, that before they die, the tortures these men will undergo under the General's direction, will make the Nazis look like school children. At the moment he prefers to watch and wait. Our men know they are under surveillance and can make no move. The damage he has already done is tremendous, but once they are brought in and made to talk . . . ' Levenson spread his hands in a hopeless gesture. 'The only card we have in our favour is the fact that the General does not know that we know.'

'But surely,' said Leigh, 'he must have written down his information or passed it on to one of his colleagues.'

This time it was Gorebain who had answered. 'No, Simon. This is the whole point. The man has a photographic memory and never writes anything important down. He boasts of his mind as the most comprehensive filing cabinet in East Germany. As for passing information to his colleagues, the man is utterly selfish and would never share his findings with anyone else in case they were to share any of the credit. It's only by something close to a miracle that we have this information at all.

'The General's position at the moment is, to say the least, a little uncertain and it is likely that he will be replaced within six months. His taste for good living and extravagant women does not fit in with his country's image however proficient the man may be. He knows full well that with one coup of this size and importance his position will be assured for a long time to come. Time is running out, Simon. We received information last week that the General is almost ready to pull in the net. That is why he must be disposed of before it is too late. Apart from the lives that would be lost, the damage that would be done to this country if our men talk, would take ten years to repair.'

As he unpacked his Revelation in his room at the Hotel Mannheim in East Berlin, Leigh wondered as he had wondered in Levenson's study what would have happened if he had refused point-blank to undertake the mission.

He was pleasantly surprised to find a bottle of scotch whisky and a box of

German cigars on the dressing-table in his room. 'They are certainly doing their best to try and make me feel at home.' He knew that Scotch was an almost unheard of luxury in East Germany. Leigh walked over to the window — in the grey street below, tin helmeted soldiers, machine guns over their shoulders, marched. He wondered idly if Germany would ever change. He remembered Berlin before the war as one of the playgrounds of the world and still found it difficult to think of two Berlins. It was like erecting a wall across the centre of London or Paris.

With his first meeting scheduled for 9.30 in the morning, Leigh decided to have a quiet drink in his room and go to bed early. He picked up the telephone from the bedside table and asked for room service. He ordered Borsch, fillet steak, salad and a lager.

After half an hour there was a knock on the door and a young waiter with close cropped fair hair and nervous darting eyes entered the room with a laden trolley. He wheeled it over to the chair beneath the window.

'Danke,' said Leigh, reaching for his wallet to tip the man.

The waiter came towards Leigh, suddenly grabbed hold of his arm and pressing his finger to his lips in a gesture of silence pulled him into the bathroom. He closed the door and turned on the shower full blast.

Putting his mouth close to a bewildered Leigh's ear he said in perfect English, 'Mr Leigh, the General's D. Day is the day after tomorrow. That's when the net comes in and the fish are caught. You must act very fast.'

Leigh pulled the man close to him. 'Tomorrow night is my D. Day,' he said.

The man seemed satisfied and nodded. He turned off the shower and stepped back into the bedroom. He went to the door.

'If there is anything else you require, Herr Leigh,' he said in German, 'please do not hesitate to ring Room Service. I hope you enjoy your dinner.'

As he left the room he pointed to the ceiling light and Leigh guessed that the microphone which he knew was somewhere in the room was concealed there.

Leigh who had recovered from his surprise at the whole episode, sat down to his dinner, wondering if his new found ally was going to prove to be an asset. The steak was tough and the beer lukewarm. Leigh left most of the meal and set to work on the Scotch, which even the East Germans could not spoil.

As he drank he thought of Suki. His darling Suki. He realized that if he was killed or caught, she would be the only person he would really miss.

'Pull yourself together, man, you are not going to be caught or killed. Don't make yourself out to be a hero. You are going to do a very simple task and return to London and forget the whole business.'

That night, Leigh slept badly. He dreamt that he was being chased down a street by soldiers with machine guns and tin helmets. Every time he thought that he had lost them they would reappear and start chasing him in another direction.

Finally at about four in the morning, Leigh could sleep no longer. He took a long, cold shower and began working on business papers related to his recent negotiations with the Belgians. He became so absorbed in this task that it was 7.30 before he put down his pen and papers, and went into the bathroom to shave.

8

Dinner is Served

True to form, it began to rain soon after Leigh came down to breakfast. Also it was bitterly cold; altogether a miserable and depressing day. The hotel restaurant reminded Leigh of the buffet at Waterloo Station, although if anything, it was larger and more impersonal. There were no more than a dozen people having breakfast — all men. Nearly all sat on their own. Leigh assumed that he would be returning to the hotel to change before dinner, but he was taking no chances. He filled his cigar case, from the cedar wood box he had brought with him, and put it in his breast pocket.

The bright red Wartburg came for him promptly at 8.45. The driver other than returning Leigh's 'Gut Morgen' said nothing on the drive from the hotel to the Ministry Offices, some five kilometres

130

away. Leigh was grateful for the silence as it gave him a chance to collect his thoughts.

The Ministry building was large and ugly. Outside the massive steel doors were stationed two soldiers. Leigh's driver escorted him into the building where Donecke was waiting.

His greeting was effusive. He enquired solicitously if Leigh had slept well, if his room was comfortable, if the hotel staff were looking after him.

When Leigh had answered all these questions to Donecke's satisfaction, he thanked him for the whisky and cigars which had been placed in his room.

'No, Herr Leigh, it is the General you must thank for that, you will have the chance tonight.'

'I look forward to it,' lied Leigh.

Donecke led the way down the corridor to a large room, comfortably furnished with a conference table and eight chairs, two at each end and three on either side. When Donecke had introduced Leigh to his five colleagues, who ranged in position from overall Production Controller of the

Computer Industry in East Berlin to a high ranking Official of the State Bank, the seven men took their places at the table, Leigh and Donecke facing each other at either end.

Three of the men present held no specific positions and were vaguely referred to by Donecke as advisers. The talks were friendly but formal. Any tension was broken at the start by Donecke who pointed to the rain outside and said, 'We have arranged this, Herr Leigh, to make you feel at home.' Everyone laughed.

Donecke then spent a considerable length of time telling Leigh that East Germany did not really want or need British computers but they were anxious to promote business relations between the two countries. Leigh let this political manoeuvring and propaganda pass without comment for some time.

At length, however, he interrupted. 'Herr Donecke, I do not wish to appear discourteous or offensive, but my business is to try and sell you computers and business machines at mutually agreeable terms. Your reasons for wanting or not wanting to buy them may be relevant to politicians but to me, as a businessman, they are not constructive or important.'

Donecke did not seem in the least concerned by this outburst. 'Naturally, Herr Leigh,' he went on, 'you are anxious to get down to essentials, I just wanted to put you in the picture, so far as my country is concerned.'

It was now the Banker's turn. In halting but correct English he came straight to the point. 'Herr Leigh, our government has allocated a considerable amount of money to purchase foreign computers and data logging equipment immediately, and thereafter subject to satisfactory progress and results from them gradually increasing annual amounts. Obviously only a percentage of this business can go to your Company, but if we can agree terms and you get in now at the beginning, there is a very real chance of your doing a considerable amount of business with the Federal Republic of East Germany within two years.'

This was the sort of straight talking

that Leigh appreciated and understood and he discussed facts and figures with the Banker for two hours. The rest of the day was spent in a welter of statistics and technical jargon interrupted only by coffee and sandwiches. Herr Donecke in his overall administrative capacity seemed content to sit back and allow the technologists, Banker and advisers to conduct the negotiations.

At five o'clock, after two hours of deadlock over the wording of the guarantees to accompany data logging equipment which the East Germans wanted to buy, agreement was provisonally reached. Price did not appear to present as much of a problem as Leigh had anticipated. But they were very specific over delivery dates, terms of guarantee, spare part replacements and other fine details.

The meeting was adjourned with a further one scheduled for the next day and as Leigh left the table he felt confident of returning to London with a good order under his belt and excellent prospects of future business. His invitation to Herr Donecke and any of his colleagues to visit his factory at some future date was greeted politely but with some reserve.

'I look forward to seeing you later at the dinner,' said the Banker, holding out his hand to Leigh. 'I am sure we will be able to do good business.'

Leigh had taken a liking to this man. 'Bankers were the same the world over. Interested in only one thing — money.'

'I hope so,' said Leigh, shaking the man's hand.

The Wartburg had obviously been assigned to him for the extent of his visit, but Leigh did not like the prolonged silences with the chauffeur. 'I am getting over sensitive,' he thought, as he relaxed in the car on the way back to the hotel. 'Because the man does not talk does not mean a thing. Perhaps he thinks I don't speak German.'

No effort had been made to disguise the fact that Leigh's room had been thoroughly and systematically searched. His shirts were in a different drawer and his toothpaste tube had been slit open. Levenson had warned him that it was more than probable that his room would be searched.

He had warned: 'Remember, because you are a foreigner you are automatically suspect.'

Leigh knew already from the incident with the waiter the previous evening that the room was wired for sound. Now he knew that his suitcase, clothing and toilet things, had been given the works. Nothing was missing.

What he did not know was that the General had originally given orders not to search his room as he knew from the report on Leigh that the man was in the clear, but at the last moment had changed his mind with his favourite phrase. 'You cannot be too careful.' Now he was sure of Leigh, really sure, the man was straight as a die. The General was looking forward to the dinner, any excuse for legitimate good food and drink was welcome. What sort of hosts would the German Federal Republic appear if they could not compete with the other capitals of Europe in hospitality?

Leigh had a long shower to try and ease

away the tensions that had now returned in full force. He was pleased with the day's work. He took great enjoyment in negotiating a hard deal and the tougher it was the more satisfaction he derived from it.

Before dressing, Leigh put a call through to his factory. He knew that Joyce would still be there and he gambled that the call would be taped and played back to Donecke.

Within five minutes Joyce was on the line.

'Hello, Donald, how are things?'

'Fine, Mr Leigh. We've had a bit of union trouble over overtime but nothing serious. How's Berlin?'

'Fine. I think we'll get a strong order here. Although there's still a lot to be discussed they're very efficient and business like.' Leigh knew that Donecke would feel pleased by this. 'I should be back in a couple of days,' he went on. 'You received the copies of the Belgian Agreement O.K.?'

'Yes, we got them this morning. We'll begin the necessary modifications next week.'

'O.K. Donald. I doubt if I'll be in touch with you before I return. If I get back on Friday, I'll be in Saturday morning as usual.'

'Right you are, Mr Leigh. See you then.'

Leigh felt satisfied that now he had told Joyce his probable date of return, on the assumption that this information would find its way back to Donecke, the Germans would think twice about detaining him after Friday without good reason. He was not a pessimist by nature but he did not like to leave things to chance.

The dinner was being held in the Ministry Building and the car was coming to pick him up at 8.30. Now the moment of truth was drawing near Leigh felt far more relaxed and confident than at any time since leaving London. His conscience which had troubled him at first had been relegated to third place behind a will for survival and a desire to succeed. The thought of the men who would die if he failed and the information that would be brutally and scientifically extracted from them before they did finally die, left no room for self-doubt in Leigh's mind.

He dressed carefully and unhurriedly in a heavy silk evening shirt and Barathea dinner suit. He had no patent leather shoes with him and settled for a pair of highly polished 'Bally' slip-ons. After double checking the cigar case, he put his Dunhill lighter in his jacket pocket and surveyed himself in the dressing mirror, half expecting to see some sign on his face that would betray his guilt. But that same cold, slightly cruel face that had left London stared unsmilingly back at him in East Berlin.

The car was punctual, as always, and apart from a brief word of greeting no words were exchanged between Leigh and the chauffeur on the short drive from the hotel to the Ministry building.

When the car pulled up outside the building, the chauffeur led the way down a broad passage towards a chandelier lit reception room on the ground floor, where cocktails and canapés were being served.

When Donecke caught sight of Leigh, he came towards him, a smile of welcome on his pale face.

'Ah, Herr Leigh. It is indeed good to see you again away from the battlefield.'

Donecke laughed loudly at his joke and taking Leigh's arm, led him to the far side of the room.

There were about forty men and women there. All impeccably dressed in evening clothes. Leigh wondered how often they had this chance to pretend that they were living normal lives in a civilized country.

'It will be impossible to introduce you to everyone, but naturally you must meet the General first. He looks forward to meeting you so much.'

Leigh followed Donecke across the room waving now and then to one of the men who had been present at the meeting earlier in the day. The Banker who was addressing a group of people around him, smiled warmly at Leigh and raised his hand in greeting.

By the French windows stood a very tall distinguished looking man in full military dress. A row of ribbons were pinned to his beautifully cut uniform. He had short iron grey hair, a long slightly hooked nose and thin cynical lips. He was smoking a cigarette through a black holder and was talking to a strikingly attractive woman of about thirty-five.

As Leigh approached, the man who he knew must unquestionably be the General turned and looked at him. His eyes which were blue in colour were cold as ice chips and held no warmth or feeling: they seemed to look right inside Leigh's mind and he felt almost hypnotized by them, unable to look away.

The General took a step forward, his carefully manicured hand outstretched towards Leigh. He did not smile.

'Mr Leigh, this is indeed a great pleasure. I have been looking forward to meeting you. I do hope Herr Donecke has been looking after you.' The spell was broken: Leigh clasped the General's hand.

The man's English was superb. He spoke in the cultured tone of a highly educated Englishman and Leigh after shaking hands with the man and exchanging the necessary pleasantries remarked on his fluency and lack of accent.

'Well, Mr Leigh, it is not surprising. I studied at your Cambridge University before the war. Some of my happiest memories are of that most beautiful English city.'

Donecke after presenting Leigh to the General slunk away, relieved no doubt at not having to make conversation with him for a while. A waiter brought a glass of champagne over to Leigh, and at the same time topped up the General's glass from the bottle of Taittinger Blanc de Blanc on his silver tray.

The General introduced Leigh to his companion who was also his current mistress. She spoke little English and Leigh conversed with her in his adequate German for some time.

'You speak good German,' said the General.

'I learnt it at school,' replied Leigh. 'And I have practised on my several trips to Germany.'

'Of course you mean the other Germany?' the General replied, smiling for the first time, and sipping his champagne.

'West Germany, yes,' answered Leigh sensing that the General was trying to provoke him and that he was treading on dangerous ground.

At that moment, to Leigh's relief, dinner was announced and the General holding his arm out for the woman, led the way into an ornate dining-room adjoining the reception room. A long, oak refectory table stretched the length of the room, with an enormous white linen table cloth draped across it. The cutlery on the table was of the finest silver and the crystal wine glasses were tinted a very faint pink.

The General indicated the chair on his left for Leigh, the woman sat on his right.

'As good as Buckingham Palace, eh?' said the General gesturing towards the opulence on the table.

It would have been very difficult to match the overall splendour of the room and table decoration anywhere and Leigh congratulated the General, who smiled in gratification.

'Believe me, Mr Leigh, it gives me great pleasure to entertain someone who really appreciates the good things of life. I am afraid many of my colleagues do not appreciate the aesthetic.'

'Poor devils,' thought Leigh, 'they're lucky if they get enough to eat half the time without worrying about silver knives and forks.'

'I love beautiful things,' the General went on. 'By good living, I do not mean over indulgence but by surrounding myself with the very finest of everything.'

When the wine had been poured by smart waiters in white starched tunics, the General stood up and raised his right hand. Within seconds the room was silent.

'Ladies and Gentlemen. I do not propose to make a long speech,' he said, 'but I must say a few words to welcome our Guest of Honour, Mr Simon Leigh, from Great Britain.

'We hope that as a result of his journey to our country, close bonds of friendship and trade will continue to develop between us. We on our part will do all we can to promote these bonds. I feel sure that Mr Leigh will agree with me that it is visits to the Republic of East Germany by businessmen such as himself which turn ideals of mutual prosperity and strength into reality.

'Let us all drink a toast to Mr Simon Leigh.'

Everybody stood up and drank the toast and Leigh smiled, slightly embarrassed by this unexpected honour. When everyone was once again seated, the General again spoke.

'I will now ask Herr Leigh to say a few words.'

Leigh, who had not been prepared for this, stood up and put down his glass. He had to be very careful what he said in this highly sensitive country.

'I hope,' he said, 'that everybody can understand my German.'

There was polite laughter.

'I can only endorse the General's words and add one thing. I on my part will do everything possible to promote an understanding between our two countries through trade and commerce. Judging by the wonderful welcome you have all given me, any Englishman would feel the same.'

Obviously he had said the right thing because everyone clapped heartily. Leigh could not think what to propose for a toast with safety but decided on 'A greater understanding and co-operation between the East European countries of the world and the West.'

He sat down.

The General leaned over to him. 'Good words, Mr Leigh. Good words.'

Dinner had begun.

9

The General

The General talked informatively and with obvious enjoyment to Leigh about England, recalling people and places he had known there. He was a sadistic, evil man, this Leigh knew but nonetheless he found himself strangely attracted to the General who was a man of undoubted intelligence and charm.

Leigh was amused by the General's questions about England. 'Was the Restaurant Manager at the Savoy Grill still Luigi? Did the men still wear morning dress for Ascot and the women their outrageous hats?' And so on.

As he spoke Leigh tried to imagine this man capable of the atrocities and tortures which Levenson had described. But looking at the thin cynical lips, the cold, hypnotic eyes, he did not find it difficult.

They spoke in German so as to include

147

the woman whose name was Erica Von Starbro in the conversation. However, she did not do much talking, in fact Leigh acquired the impression that she was afraid of the General. She smiled at his slightest joke and kept her eyes fixed to his face while he was speaking.

'Well, Mr Leigh,' said the General, after a short lapse in the conversation, 'how do you find our country? Very few of your compatriots have had the privilege of visiting it.'

'It is very interesting, Herr General,' said Leigh, determined that he was not going to allow himself to be provoked by the General.

The General looked closely at him, his eyes penetrating and searching. His face was ruddier than before and Leigh guessed that he had consumed a fair amount of drink before dinner, as well as the several glasses of wine he had drunk in Leigh's presence.

'How do you feel,' the General went on, 'knowing that your country is not and never can be a major world power again? Such a fact would, I am sure, make me feel very ashamed.'

Leigh, who was not accustomed to playing the part of a diplomat, was not going to say anything to upset the dinner in the slightest way.

'I leave those sort of problems to the politicians,' he answered amicably. 'I am a businessman, and believe me, Herr General, that is a full time occupation.'

The General nodded the subject aside, realizing perhaps that Leigh's temper was not going to be aroused.

'You are not married, Mr Leigh?'

'Was that a question or statement of fact,' wondered Leigh.

'No, my wife is dead.'

'That is a great shame. There are some very attractive women in this country, you know.' He leered drunkenly at his companion and pinched her cheek, none too gently. She smiled nervously, but said nothing.

As the crêpes Suzettes were being served, the General pushed back his chair and rose unsteadily to his feet; silence fell over the room once more. He raised his wine glass, which had been refilled yet again.

'Ladies and Gentlemen,' he said shakily, 'I give you the Federal Republic of East Germany.'

Leigh drank the toast politely along with his German companions. Donecke seated far down the table exchanged a worried glance with the man in the green uniform seated on his right. He was concerned that the General was going to make a scene. It would not be the first time. But the General seemed to suddenly sober up and by the time brandy was served, he was his usual composed self once again.

Leigh listened to the man on his left, who was telling him somewhat sheepishly that he had not tasted brandy for more than a year.

'Of course,' he added hurriedly catching the General's eye, 'I could have had it any time, but I am a beer drinker really.'

'Of course,' agreed Leigh.

The General interrupted the man in the middle of a sentence to draw Leigh's attention. 'You must try a German cigar,

Mr Leigh. They are quite as good as the Dutch.'

Leigh smiled and took the cigar.

'Thank you. In return you must have one of my cigars.' He took from the cigar case the Romeo y Julieta, fractionally shorter in length than the two cigars on either side of it.

The General took the cigar and sniffed it appreciatively then he rubbed it gently to his ear in the manner of a connoisseur, to test the condition.

'There is one thing I really miss, Mr Leigh, and that is a good Havana after dinner. Although we are very friendly with Cuba, they are not readily available in this country. Of course, they are completely prohibited in America,' he added, with spiteful satisfaction. When he had lit up, he dipped the end of the cigar into his brandy glass to get the taste of the brandy throughout the cigar, he explained to Frau Von Starbro, who had been watching him, a slightly puzzled expression on her lovely face.

'I will send you a box of Romeos from Dunhills when I return to London,' said

Leigh. The cigar the General had given him was quite the coarsest he had ever smoked, but he made no comment and steeled himself to smoke it to the bitter end.

'That would indeed be a most welcome gift,' beamed the General, sitting back contentedly and luxuriating in the cloud of rich Havana which swirled around his aristocratic face like smoke encircling a ship's funnel.

Leigh had asked Levenson what would happen if the General refused the cigar.

'The General will not refuse,' Levenson had replied with certainty. 'Within two hours of finishing the cigar, he will be dead. Half-way down, concealed in the leaf, is a minute sac. Once the heat from the cigar bursts the surface of the sac, a fatally potent gas will be released. Every puff the General takes on his cigar will take him one step nearer the grave. The gas is undetectable either by taste or smell and the General will notice nothing different in the flavour of the cigar. Within a short while of his finishing the cigar, the poison will have thoroughly circulated his blood stream and his heart will no longer be able to push the blood around. His death will have the symptoms of a coronary thrombosis and if a postmortem should be performed, there will be nothing to prove otherwise. It's too good a death for him,' Levenson had finished. 'Far too good.'

★ ★ ★

People began to leave soon, and all without exception, insisted on shaking Leigh's hand. One of the last to leave was a tall man in a green uniform whom the General introduced as his deputy, Colonel Muller.

He was a short unimpressive man of medium build, but something in his appearance struck Leigh. It was not until later, that he realized what it was. Despite the man's lack of size he gave an impression of immense strength and power. Leigh could imagine him taking pleasure in assisting the General in some of his more 'painful' duties.

When there were only half a dozen

people left at the table, the General held forth to these die-hards or sycophants about the evils of the capitalist system of banking. The brandy had turned his pale complexion quite scarlet. Leigh caught the eyes of the Banker who winked at him as if to say 'listen to Rothschild'.

Leigh took advantage of a temporary lull in the conversation to stand up and say his farewells. The General seemed disappointed that he was leaving so soon.

'Herr General, I have had a wonderful evening and I have thoroughly enjoyed it, but I have to be fresh for the morning otherwise I won't be able to match the wits of Herr Donecke and his colleagues at the negotiating table.'

Everyone laughed and Donecke who was inevitably still there, rose to accompany Leigh to his car, but the General stopped him with a raised hand. 'I shall personally escort Herr Leigh.'

Leigh said goodbye to the Banker and followed the General to the heavy steel doors of the building where the General, who now seemed completely recovered from the effects of the alcohol he had consumed, stopped and placed his hand on Leigh's shoulder. Again the pale blue eyes seemed to probe his very being.

'Mr Leigh, it has been refreshing to meet a civilized man. You know, a man of your abilities and intelligence might well be able to be of service to me, in a business capacity of course,' he added quickly. 'We must talk again privately in my office before you leave for London.'

Leigh, who wanted to retain the General's favour to the end, smiled. 'I would like that very much, Herr General.'

'Good. Well, good night and remember, anything you want, just get in touch with me.'

'Thank you once again for your hospitality.'

'It was a great pleasure to meet you. I hope to see you again very soon.'

* * *

Leigh had not realized how tired he was and he fell asleep in the car. The driver woke him when they arrived at the hotel. Leigh thanked the man and walked to the lift, certain that he was by no means out of the wood yet.

He, too, had had a lot to drink and he took a couple of Alka Seltzers before going to bed. Tired as he was, sleep did not come easily. It was still difficult to believe that the General would die as a result of the dinner. That he, Simon Leigh, businessman turned agent, had killed him in cold blood with no chance or warning. Subtly, ingeniously with an innocent cigar.

'Spy is a dirty word'. The true meaning of Levenson's words hit Leigh. Whatever atrocities the General had committed, however evil he was, he had done Leigh no harm. On the contrary, he had entertained him, talked with him, laughed with him. The attraction Leigh had felt for the man was wrong and he knew it. There was no room for those sort of feelings in this business. But how would he feel, he wondered, in a year, or ten years time, knowing that he had gone to East Berlin to sell computers and had at a dinner in his honour, murdered his host in cold blood, as surely as if he had stuck a knife in his back.

Leigh's thoughts turned to Suki with whom he had fallen in love. Simon Leigh, who since his wife's death had played it cool with women, always polite but never more. Detached, hard, Simon Leigh was finally hooked.

Leigh had made up his mind that he would ask Suki to marry him when he got back to London; he was sure she would accept. Would he tell her what he had done or would he keep it inside him for the rest of his life. Where would they live? Leigh's flat suited him as a bachelor, but once more married he would perhaps buy a mews house and the dream yacht would become a reality.

Leigh had not felt so excited about anything outside his business for a long time. He closed his eyes and imagined himself with Suki on his arm walking in Hyde Park on a warm Sunday morning. Lunch at a pub. Dinner in a little Chelsea bistro.

All these thoughts came tumbling through his sleep-starved brain.

Then the cold fear which had never

been far away during the past few days crept back. 'This is always supposing that you return to England,' a voice kept repeating inside him.

* * *

After what seemed hours, sleep came to Simon Leigh, but not for long. In his sub-conscious, sleep befuddled mind, he heard rifle shots, one after the other, clear and sharp, louder and louder. He awoke, his body bathed in perspiration.

Someone was trying to break down the door.

'Herr Leigh, Herr Leigh, let us in.' Leigh staggered from the bed and grabbed his bathrobe. His head ached abominably.

He threw open the door, furious at having been deprived of his sleep. Fear, as yet, having no place in his mind.

'What the bloody hell do you want barging in here at this time of the night.'

Donecke and two military policemen, their hands on their machine guns stood facing him.

'Herr Leigh, we are sorry to disturb you, but something very terrible has occurred. The General, he is dead.'

Leigh's sleep filled mind genuinely registered shock and surprise at this news.

'My God,' he said, headache and temper temporarily forgotten. 'When? What happened?'

'Soon after leaving the banquet. While he was in the car on the way back to his apartment, he collapsed. On arrival at the hospital he was found to be dead. They think he had a coronary thrombosis.'

Leigh was now wide awake and alert. 'Careful,' he told himself, 'Very careful.'

He looked coldly at Donecke and spoke quietly.

'With the greatest respect, Herr Donecke, and sorry as I am to hear this terrible news, I'd like to know why you have come to my hotel in the middle of the night with these two Gestapo thugs.' He indicated the two leather clad policemen, whose eyes had not moved from his since he had opened the door. 'Surely to God it could have waited until morning.'

This outburst had the desired affect on Donecke, who looked embarrassed and sheepish.

'Herr Leigh, I am truly sorry, but I have had orders from my superiors that you are to be taken to police headquarters for an interview. If it had been left to me, I would have waited until the morning, but you understand how it is. I have to obey my orders like anyone else.'

Leigh had been warned that routine questioning would be on the cards for him and he knew that it would be fatal for him to refuse to go. 'Of course,' he said more kindly to Donecke. 'I must get dressed. Perhaps your two companions could wait outside the door.'

Donecke looked doubtful, but he gave an order and the two policemen left the room, somewhat reluctantly Leigh thought.

'This must have been a terrible shock for you too, Herr Donecke,' said Leigh, pulling on his trousers. He poured out two stiff whiskies from the bottle the General had sent him. Donecke took the glass gratefully and drank the whisky down in one gulp.

While Leigh was dressing he thought about trying to get a message to his waiter, but he decided that it was very unlikely that the man would be on duty at this hour and even if he was it would look highly suspicious ringing Room Service now even if he could think of a way of passing a message. He discarded the idea and after a final quick drink left the room with Donecke. The two policemen had replaced their machine guns over their shoulders but their hands hung nervously at their sides.

No one spoke in the lift and on the walk across the hotel foyer the few hotel staff still on duty kept their eyes firmly on the ground as if in the presence of a funeral procession. This Gestapo treatment was making Leigh feel more nervous than he would have admitted, and the whisky which he had drunk to try and gain some Dutch courage merely served to increase his headache.

When he was seated in the back of a black Wartburg with the two policemen on either side of him and Donecke in front with the driver, he kept repeating to himself the words which Levenson had tried to impress upon him — they were not a great consolation in his present plight but they made sense.

'Remember, Simon,' Levenson had said, 'if they do take you in for questioning which is more than probable, it is not because they necessarily suspect foul play but they are a suspicious lot of bastards by nature and if they could somehow tie you in with the General's death, it would have tremendous propaganda value for them. Keep calm and answer all their questions as truthfully as possible. Whatever you do, don't panic — for everybody's sake.'

Leigh made a conscious effort to relax, as he had been taught in the Commandos, tensing and untensing the muscles throughout his body, starting with his feet and working up to his head. It did not help a great deal, but when the car came to a standstill outside the same Ministry building where he had spent the day negotiating and the evening wining and dining, Leigh felt calm, if not confident enough, to answer any questions.

10

Colonel Muller

News of the General's death had obviously spread like wildfire despite the hour. The Ministry building was a hive of activity with electric lights blazing in every office window.

Two soldiers had been stationed outside the doors, where a few hours before Leigh had said his farewells to the General. The two policemen who had escorted Leigh from the hotel, ushered him down a narrow stone corridor where he had not been before. Donecke followed behind, his steel tipped heels echoing importantly.

They came to a staircase, which the policemen gestured for Leigh to ascend. On the first floor was a row of doors with no name on any of them.

Donecke ordered the policemen to wait. He knocked on one of the doors, indistinguishable in appearance from any of the others.

'Enter,' said a voice from within.

Donecke turned the handle and gestured for Leigh to go in. The two policemen stood in the doorway waiting.

The room was furnished with the bare necessities of any office. A desk, black telephone, three chairs and steel filing cabinet. There was no carpet on the floor. Behind the desk, which was empty save for a single pink folder sat Colonel Muller. Even from a sitting position the impression Leigh had gained at the dinner — of a man utterly ruthless and cruel was reinforced. He was wearing the same green uniform that he had been wearing earlier.

'You may go,' said Muller to Donecke and the two policemen, who were hovering uncertainly in the doorway.

When the door had shut, Leigh stood waiting for the Colonel to speak, but he sat silent and motionless behind the desk, save for his fingers which beat a ceaseless tattoo on the arms of the chair. He studied Leigh for several minutes without speaking.

Leigh returned his gaze evenly. He had had some experience of the various methods of interrogation in his Commando training and knew that this unnatural silence was intended to break down his barriers and increase his fear. The counter method was not to react.

'We meet again, Mr Leigh. So soon,' said the man, at last in heavily accented English.

Still Leigh said nothing.

'Do you speak German?' Muller asked.

'Enough to get by,' Leigh replied.

'Good. We will speak in German. Please take a seat.'

Leigh sat down making an effort to look unconcerned.

'You seem to have landed yourself in trouble, Mr Leigh,' said Muller matter of factly. He leaned forward, his short fingers stopped their drumming.

'I'm afraid I don't understand you,' said Leigh in a puzzled voice. 'What do you mean trouble?'

'Come now, Mr Leigh. Let us not play

games. You were the only person to be completely alone with the General the whole evening. He escorted you from the dining hall to the front door. Two hours later, he was dead. The implications, Mr Leigh, are obvious even to a fool, which I don't think for one moment, that you are.'

Muller's voice was pleasant — almost conspiratorial.

'Herr Donecke told me the General died of a heart attack,' said Leigh.

Muller shrugged this idea away. 'It seems to be the opinion of most of the idiots around here that that is the case. I think differently, Mr Leigh.'

Muller's habit of calling him Mr Leigh after every sentence was unnerving Leigh.

'Surely the doctors can confirm it,' said Leigh.

'Huh,' sneered the man. 'I don't care what anybody says. I knew the General. I worked with him every day, played tennis with him, drank with him. The man had the constitution of a lion.'

'It is often those strongest and least susceptible in theory that get heart attacks,' said Leigh.

The man ignored this remark. Again he sat silent for several moments. When he spoke again the friendliness had disappeared from his voice — now it was the menacing voice of a man trying hard to control his anger.

'Mr Leigh, let us stop this verbal war-game. I want to know exactly what happened when you left the dining hall with the General.'

Obediently Leigh repeated the conversation he had had with the General, truthfully and in detail.

When he had finished Muller picked up the folder from his desk and opened it.

'Mr Leigh, if I'm the only person in East Berlin who thinks so, I am convinced that the General did not die of a heart attack. How he died and why may never be known but as far as who is concerned I am equally convinced that you are the murderer.'

Leigh fought to control the sound of his voice. He wished now that he had drunk more whisky before leaving the hotel. His already stretched nerves were like taut wires almost at breaking point.

'I resent your accusations most strongly,' he said, in a voice which thankfully came out normal. 'When I return to Britain I shall protest in no uncertain measure about these diabolical and utterly unfounded allegations.'

'Mr Leigh,' replied Muller, smiling for the first time. 'I would point out that apart from it being by no means certain that you will be returning to Britain, as your Government will not give us official representation in London, protesting can achieve nothing.'

'Touché,' thought Leigh, wondering if Muller was really as convinced about his guilt as he claimed — or if he was trying to bluff the truth out of him.

'I have in front of me,' Muller continued, indicating the pink folder, 'an interesting and enlightening document. It is what we call a Personal Class A.100 report, Mr Leigh. The subject of the report is yourself and there is not much about you that it misses.' Again the small mean mouth twisted into the semblance of a smile. 'If it is accurate of which I have no doubt, it means one of two things.

'Either you are a legitimate businessman on a legitimate business trip to East Berlin — or . . . ' Muller paused dramatically before going on, 'or you are hiding under the cover of a legitimate businessman on a legitimate business trip to East Berlin, while at the same time playing the role of assassin. The latter is my personal assessment of you. I believe that you were sent here by your government with the sole purpose of assassinating the General. Right or wrong, I will discover the truth. Of that, my dear Mr Leigh, you need have no doubt.

'It may interest you to see this. Human vanity is such that a man always likes to read what others say about him.'

Muller pushed the pink folder containing several sheets of neatly typed foolscap across the desk.

Leigh hesitated before picking it up. He was calmer and more resolute than at any time since entering the office. They would have to kill him before he confessed to anything. He half-wished now that he had accepted the suicide pill that Levenson had offered him.

'In the unlikely event that you should be tortured, Simon, it's always best to be prepared.'

But he had stubbornly refused, insisting that the less he carried with him of an incriminating nature, the safer he was.

He picked up the pink folder and opened it. He read the heading.

Name   Simon Leigh.
Report   Class A.100 (Personal)
Agent   49003 (Brussels XRP)

'Brussels!' A constricting physical pain as sharp and real as if he had been kicked, gripped his chest making breathing difficult. He felt the blood drain from his face.

The man behind the desk watched him closely, his eyes alert.

As he began reading about himself, facts and details so personal as to be like looking into a verbal mirror, Leigh prayed against the reality which had struck him like a thunderbolt that it was not true

— that there must be some other explanation, but when he read the words 'sexually proficient' there could be no possible shadow of doubt.

Suki, his darling Suki, who had made him feel good by taking such a deep interest in him, who had made him move to her apartment so that she could get to know him better. Suki, to whom he had given himself completely for the first and only time since Klaire. To whom he had given his trust, his love. Leigh forgot Muller sitting not four feet away from him, forgot the General, forgot Levenson, forgot Gorebain. What an utterly blind, gullible fool he had been. How easily he had been taken in, deceived and finally betrayed by the beautiful girl with the long black hair and sad grey eyes.

Leigh let the report drop to the floor and made no attempt to pick it up. He closed his eyes and sat very still, his fists clenched so tightly that the blood drained out of them and the knuckles showed marble white. There was no heating in the room and it was not warm, but Leigh felt sweat break out all over his body. He tried to speak, but the saliva which had accumulated in his mouth, made him choke. It was some time before he stopped coughing.

The pain in his chest intensified until he thought he was going to black out.

Muller had observed Leigh's behaviour in near astonishment. He had not realized that the girl would have such an effect on Leigh. The General had joked with him.

'Let's hope that he at least likes Suki enough to go to bed with her and talk about himself a little.'

It was five minutes before Leigh managed to control himself enough to speak. As he asked the question he realized the stupidity of it, but he had to know for certain. 'She works for you in Brussels?'

'Of course, Mr Leigh. She did not just send us this report out of kindness.' Muller stood up. As the light caught his face Leigh saw that his bulging eyes were very bloodshot as if he, too, had had little sleep. He came and sat on the front of the desk, his face close to Leigh's, his breath stank of beer and Leigh nearly vomited.

'The time for games is over, my friend. Here in this room, either with or without your co-operation, I intend to find out the truth. There is no question of fair-play, no rules, no British justice. The easier you make it for me, the easier I'll make it for you, but I warn you that I will go to any lengths . . . ' again he paused to add drama to his words, 'any lengths whatsoever, to extract the truth from you.'

Muller did not add that once he had extracted his confession from Leigh, he was not unduly bothered whether it was true or false.

Levenson had been right. The propaganda value from such a confession would be invaluable to East Germany, and could not fail to add to its bargaining power in the game of world politics. More important to Muller, it would almost certainly guarantee his position as the General's successor. He stood up and walked around the room, his face thoughtful.

'Somehow, Mr. Leigh. In the short time you were alone with the General at the end of the banquet you administered some poison to him which resulted in his death. It is my intention to find out how you performed this ingenious murder without his knowing.'

'Very close,' thought Leigh, his mind still numbed with shock and disbelief about Suki. 'But not quite close enough.'

'That's ridiculous. I've told you. I was only alone with him for a couple of minutes. Anyway, why on earth should I want to kill him.'

'Something else I intend to find out before very long.'

He came over and sat once again on the desk in front of Leigh, his voice now pleasant and friendly again.

'Really, Mr Leigh, I hate violence, it's so uncivilized — don't you agree? If you would only tell me the truth it would save a lot of unpleasantness for both of us.' He smiled disarmingly.

'I have told you the truth,' shouted Leigh angrily. 'I am a businessman who came here at your Government's invitation, to try and do business and promote trade between our two countries. Because the General has a heart attack and dies while I happen to be here, I am accused of murder and God knows what else. No wonder no one trusts you bloody Communists or wants to visit your countries.'

The smile disappeared from Muller's face as if he had been struck. He raised his arm and brought it down with all his force on Leigh's face. The metal bracelet strap of his watch caught on Leigh's mouth and blood started to trickle from the gash that appeared immediately.

'Do not ever shout at me again,' said Muller trying hard to control his own voice.

Blindly and without thinking, Leigh grabbed the man's fat neck, and punched him as hard as he could on the throat. At the sound of the struggle, the two policemen, who must have stationed themselves outside the door, rushed in and while one of them pulled Leigh off Muller, the other clubbed him savagely on the shoulders and arms with his revolver until he fell to the floor: even then the policemen continued to beat him with the butt of the revolver, until Leigh's body was a mass of blood and bruises.

Muller choked for several minutes as he tried to regain his breath. Gradually he recovered enough to speak. He rose to his feet, angrily shaking off the arms of the policemen who made to assist him.

Leigh, who was still lying motionless on the floor, noted with satisfaction that Muller's throat had turned a deep purple and that blood was running from his chin which had struck the floor as he fell. He attempted to rise, but found that he could not move his arms; he fell back to the floor exhausted.

Suddenly, with no warning, Muller came towards Leigh and kicked him viciously in the kidney. Leigh grunted with pain and blacked out. In the split second before complete unconsciousness descended, he thought he heard the sound of a telephone shrilly ringing in his subconscious.

When he came to, he was still lying on the hard floor, his mouth and nose, so caked with congealed blood that breathing was difficult. He was in agony from the clubbing he had received on the shoulders and arms and from the kick in his back. He tried to focus his eyes on Muller who was seated once again at his desk, but the effort was too much and he closed his eyes. Leigh wondered how long he had been unconscious.

'Can you hear me, Leigh?' asked Muller, his voice very soft as if it hurt him to speak. 'I will deal with your recent performance later. For the moment there are more important matters to attend to. I have received instructions that if I have not extracted a signed confession from you by daybreak, that I am to release you.' He glanced at his watch, whose bracelet was stained red with blood. 'That leaves me four hours. Two hundred and forty minutes. It is not a long time, but it is long enough. With time and truth drugs there would be no difficulty, but four hours does not leave long enough for these more subtle methods of interrogation. If we were to physically torture you with any guaranteed results, it would also take longer than four hours. To extract a confession from you, there is, however, a way, which thanks to the General's foresight, will, I am sure, prove effective.

'I will give you one last chance, Mr Leigh. I have a statement here — sign it and fill in the missing details — and you can walk out of this office a free man.'

'Go to hell,' croaked Leigh, the effort of speaking made him nearly black out again.

Muller nodded to one of the policemen, who left the room. Leigh felt as if he would never get up again, but then he was not sure that he really wanted to. He lay on the floor, his eyes closed. Wishing unconsciousness would return, anything but this pain. After what seemed only a second, he heard the door open again and footsteps.

'Both of you get out,' Muller ordered the two policemen.

Leigh heard the two men march over to the door and leave the room. He knew that they would not be far away.

Leigh tried to turn. Slowly, painfully, he moved his head. As he turned, there was a gasp from the direction of the door. With supreme effort he turned his head right round and opened his eyes. Through hazily focusing eyes, he saw Suki. Beautiful, in a simple white dress, she stood framed in the doorway looking down at him, a look of terror on her face. Around her neck was the heavy gold chain. Her lips to his blurred eyes were a slash of shocking pink.

After a moment of stunned silence she came towards Leigh and kneeling beside his body, she cradled his bloody face in her arms. He opened his eyes long enough to see that her face was wet with tears. He wanted to speak, to tell her to leave him alone, to call her every foul name under the sun, to abuse her, to hurt her, but he could not form the words. This time it was not the pain that prevented him.

As if reading his mind, she bent very close to him and put her mouth to his ear. 'I am so sorry, *chéri*,' she whispered, trying to restrain her sobbing enough to get the words out, 'some day, you will understand and perhaps even forgive me. Please, please do not hate me.'

'Enough of this touching tenderness,' snapped Muller officiously. 'Fräulein

179

Laval, as you know, the General brought you here to entertain him. Because of his unfortunate and untimely death you have an even more beneficial task to perform for the State. Using you, I intend to get a signed confession of murder from your friend and lover, Simon Leigh.'

The girl stopped sobbing and through tear-filled eyes stared in amazement at Muller.

'Are you crazy?' asked the girl in genuine astonishment. 'Leigh murder the General. Didn't you read my report?'

Muller lit a cigarette before replying.

'I read your report. Whether he did it or not is irrelevant to me. Leigh is going to confess. My plans have had to be slightly revised by the lack of time permitted. You, Fräulein, are going to be the instrument for the extraction of the confession from Leigh. You have in the past been useful to us, but you're beginning to slip. We cannot afford mistakes. Also, your obvious involvement with this man, who was given to you purely as a routine assignment is not to be tolerated.'

Muller reached under his desk and pressed a buzzer. The two policemen immediately entered the room, their machine guns at the ready. Muller pointed to Leigh on the floor.

'Place him in a chair.'

When Leigh had been dragged semi-conscious along the floor and slumped into a chair, Muller came towards him, a glass of water, which had appeared from somewhere, in his hand.

'Drink this,' he snapped, any trace of friendliness gone from his voice.

Leigh needed no second invitation and trying to steady his hand enough to hold the glass still, he drank the water greedily. He felt slightly better and could just manage to keep his eyes open without too much pain now. His body felt broken in several places. He stared at Suki, who had stopped crying, hating her for what she had done and despising himself for being taken in so easily.

One of the policemen produced some rope and tied Leigh's two shattered arms and legs to the chair making movement impossible. Not that he could have moved anyway.

When Leigh was trussed like a chicken, Muller sat back in his chair and smiled. 'Strip the girl,' he ordered. His eyes did not leave Leigh's face as the two policemen, roughly and with unconcealed pleasure tore the white dress from the girl's body.

Suki, who knew the kind of people she was up against made no move to resist, but placed her hands proudly on her hips and looked disdainfully at Muller.

'You are an animal,' she spat. 'Worse than an animal.' Her eyes were ablaze with hate.

The man laughed. 'You should be used to being naked in public by now, my dear,' he said, as one of the policemen ripped her brassiere off without bothering to unfasten the hook. Then her pants and stockings. They did not remove the gold necklace from around her neck.

To Leigh's mind so distorted with pain that several times he was on the verge of unconsciousness, there was something almost theatrical about the scene being enacted before him. A beautiful girl whom he had loved, standing naked save for a gold chain around her neck, was about to suffer for a crime that he had committed, but could not confess to and of which she believed him to be innocent.

Poetic justice? Perhaps, but he would not have wished Muller on his worst enemy and whatever Suki had done to him . . .

'Tie her to the other chair.'

Muller's voice brought an end to Leigh's punch-drunk dreams.

When the girl was bound facing Leigh, Muller rose from his chair and came round the desk to Leigh.

'Mr Leigh, if you sign this confession the girl will be released and set free. If you do not, or until you do, the girl will suffer a great deal of pain and humiliation.'

Leigh said nothing. He realized for the first time that Levenson and Gorebain must have known full well that there had been very little chance of his ever leaving East Berlin alive.

'Sign nothing, Simon,' whispered Suki. 'Whatever they may do to me, do not confess to a crime that you did not commit.'

'It was ironical really,' thought Leigh. 'The girl was convinced that he was innocent and even Muller was not certain of his guilt.'

'Very well, Mr Leigh, we must proceed,' said Muller, his voice silky soft.

Muller came towards the girl taking from his green uniform a heavy leather belt with a large brass buckle at the end.

'Stand by the door,' he ordered the two policemen, who were both grinning in anticipation.

Suki's eyes never left Simon's face as Muller raised the belt and brought it down with all his strength on her breasts, buckle end first. Blood started to spurt from the ugly red welts that appeared there.

'Stop it,' croaked Leigh. 'For God's sake, stop it.'

'As soon as you confess to your crime,' said Muller, raising the belt again.

'Confess to nothing, Simon. Nothing,'

Suki hissed through gritted teeth, her clear eyes dimmed with pain and the will to resist.

Again the belt fell, this time across her thighs. Despite the effort she was making to control herself, she screamed involuntarily. Again and again the belt fell on the girl, until no part of her body was unmarked.

Muller had worked himself up into an intensity of uncontrollable fervour.

'I will sign anything,' gasped Leigh. 'Leave the girl alone.' The sight of her disfigured body which had given him so much pleasure and of which she had been so proud sickened him beyond all measure. What she had done to him was forgotten for the moment.

'That is better,' said Muller, laying the belt across the desk, half disappointed at having to curtail his pleasure.

Suki, whose breath was coming in agonized gasps tried to speak.

'S-s-s-Simon, c-c-confess to nothing, I p-promise y-you that i-i-if I am not killed now, I will b-be later. I-I-I know these people, k-know their methods. Ad-admit

185

to nothing,' she implored. 'Y-you will not be saving my l-life if you do.'

Muller angrily snatched the belt from the desk and cracked it down viciously on Suki's nipples, already scarlet with blood from earlier wounds.

Muller gestured to the two policemen. 'Come here, you.'

The two men marched forward.

He pointed to Suki. 'You may have her. Do whatever you wish with her, but do not kill her.'

The men laughed with pleasure as they rested their machine guns against the desk. They began to touch Suki's broken body, roughly and cruelly. One of them put his fist between her legs forcing them apart. The girl screamed and spat in his face. The other picked up the Colonel's bloody belt from the desk and began to whip her. Saliva drooled from his mouth as he began to lose control of himself. Everytime the belt descended was like a gunshot to Leigh's tortured mind.

Muller sat there motionless a smile frozen on his face, his eyes unblinking were riveted to the girl's face. Leigh knew that he could not hold out much longer, although what Suki had said was undoubtedly true and she would die whether he confessed or not, he could not bear to watch these savages beating and torturing her any more. He could not understand why she had betrayed him, but that did not matter for now.

As to his being released, Leigh was long passed caring. He did not believe that they would let him go whether he confessed or not. He knew too much now. If it was he that was being tortured, he knew that he would never confess but this was different. Seeing this beautiful girl, that he had loved and had thought loved him being reduced to a mutilated animal by these sadistic barbarians was more than he could take. Let him admit he had killed the General. He would never tell them why.

He summoned his last reserves of strength in a desperate bid to gain Muller's attention. One of the policemen was raising his arm with the belt. As he brought it down with all his strength on the girl's raw bleeding shoulder, Leigh spoke. 'I will confess,' he began, clenching his fists painfully with the effort of trying to get the words out between split lips.

Suddenly from Suki's lips came the sound of a nut being cracked. She looked at Leigh, her eyes momentarily bright and clear again.

'I am sorry, *chéri*,' she whispered. 'I loved you truly.'

The belt fell again, but Suki did not move. Her face, white and damp with perspiration had fallen on to her chest. Muller rushed up from the desk, his pig eyes blazing with anger and frustration. He had been so close, so very close. In a few seconds he knew that he would have had his signed confession. He stamped his foot furiously on the floor, again and again.

One of the policemen forced the girl's mouth open. The pungent odour of bitter almonds pervaded the room.

'She has taken the suicide pill, Herr Colonel. She must have had it with her when she came in.'

Leigh looked at the girl's face beautiful even in death. He would only remember her body as he had known it. Not the cold corpse slumped lifeless in the chair, scarred and blood-stained.

What had she meant, he wondered. 'Some day you will understand and perhaps even forgive me.'

He looked up at Muller desperately slapping Suki's face, knowing full well it was too late. 'You'll be sorry for this, you bastard. You'll be sorry,' he shouted, finding hidden reserves of strength.

With one stride, the man was at Leigh's side, punching him uncontrollably again and again on the face and head. After the second blow unconsciousness mercifully descended upon Simon Leigh.

* * *

Harold Leveson left his basement office and walked along the corridor to a steel door with a metal plaque bearing the title 'Communications'. A wireless operator was furiously twiddling frequency knobs on an enormous receiver which stretched the length of one wall. Gorebain was

189

sitting in a leather swivel chair, chain-smoking.

The Communications officer looked up as Levenson entered, but the fat man gestured for him to continue: the Intelligence Chief consulted his Jaeger-le-Coultre watch on its wide 18 carat gold bracelet — five to six. Dawn would be breaking over London.

At exactly six o'clock there was a sudden crackle of static, then a voice, soft but clear, came over the air:

JEMIMA CALLING THERESA.
JEMIMA CALLING THERESA.

The operator adjusted a knob and a red light came on.

THERESA RECEIVING OK PROCEED.

There was a pause and then the voice continued in the same monotonous tone:

UNCLE HAS HAD A FATAL ACCIDENT DEAR BOY IS UNDERGOING HIS EXAMINATION RESULT STILL UNKNOWN.

190

The voice stopped abruptly and suddenly everyone in the room was aware of an unnerving silence. Gorebain looked at Levenson, who was still standing by the door, his face expressionless.

★　★　★

In East Berlin, not far from the Hotel Mannheim, British Agent 109 unhurriedly and with great care dismantled the radio transmitter in his small, sparsely furnished bed-sitter. When he had finished he placed what was now a perfectly normal radio on the cheap coffee table before him. He adjusted a screw at the back, then turned it on in time to hear Radio Moscow's daily news summary. When 109 had heard how the Americans had suffered severe casualties in Vietnam, that the Israelis had been guilty of shelling Jordanian civil outposts and had killed eight children, and how Russia's 'true friend and ally Egypt had warned Israel that any further trouble or unwarranted provocation would result in a major war' he switched off the radio.

Slowly, the man dressed in black trousers, white shirt and bow tie; he put on his coat as it was still very cold, and unlocking the door he went outside. He walked briskly the three blocks to the hotel, where he proceeded to set the tables in the Dining Room for breakfast.

11

Ignorance is Bliss

Dawn had not long broken over East Berlin, and although the sun was making a brave effort to radiate some degree of warmth it was still bitterly cold. Those fortunate enough to possess them, wore long sheepskin coats to work, the fleece lined collars turned right up to protect the ears, which seemed to suffer most.

The noise of the impact as the car hit the tree could be heard three blocks away. It seemed to echo for several minutes.

One man, who worked in a butcher's shop, could not erase the thought of it from his mind all day, but he did not mention it to anyone until he returned home to his two-roomed apartment that evening. His wife could see he was dying to tell her something because his right eye was twitching furiously, a sure sign that he had something on his mind.

'Did you hear it?' he asked, as soon as he had washed the smell of the cheap meat from his hands. Somehow the apartment always smelt like a butcher's shop. It was an unpleasant smell that lingered in his rough denim shirts, despite frequent washings.

'Hear what?' she called, setting down a loaf of black bread and some dripping on the table.

'Why, the car crash this morning, as I was going off to work.'

'Of course I heard it,' she answered scornfully. 'I'd have had to be deaf to have missed it. I dressed immediately and went down to see if I could help, but by the time I got there the police had arrived and they sent everybody home.'

'It was a very peculiar affair,' the man said, as if to himself, spreading the thick dripping on the bread and taking an enormous mouthful. 'I was just coming round the corner by the shoe shop when I heard what I thought was an explosion. It reminded me of the war with bombs dropping all over the place. Then as I came to the street by the park I saw the

194

car — or what was left of it. It couldn't have been more than a couple of minutes after it hit the tree. It was a government car, you know,' the man added sensing that his wife's interest was flagging. 'I could tell from the number plate, which somehow had escaped damage.'

'So what is so strange about a Government Official having an accident?' she enquired drily. 'They're not immortal you know. If you ask me, it's good riddance. One less.'

'No, its not that,' said the man softly, putting the bread down on the table and looking up. 'But when the car hit the tree there was no one in it.'

The woman said nothing for a moment. 'Are you off your head Hermann Tannlar,' she cried. 'A driverless car hit a tree?' She tapped her head contemptuously. 'Either you're mad or drunk, and if you're drunk, I would like to know where you got the money to buy the beer from.'

The man ignored his wife's outburst, but continued in the same quiet tone.

'Very soon after the crash, four soldiers

came running towards the wreckage from an army truck parked just along the street. They were carrying two bodies.'

His wife put the kettle which she was filling, down on the stove. She wiped her hands on her apron and came over to her husband, all trace of mockery gone from her face.

'What happened then?' she asked incredulously.

'They placed the bodies in the car,' her husband continued. 'One was a man's, they put his body in the driver's seat: they had to force open the door, it was so smashed in. The other was a woman's. A woman with long, black hair. From what I could see of her she must have been very beautiful. They put her in the passenger seat.'

'They were both dead?' asked the woman, lowering her voice, to a whisper.

Her husband shrugged. 'How should I know? Neither of them moved. As soon as I saw the soldiers I hid in a doorway.

'It does not do to meddle,' he added. 'Within two minutes an ambulance had arrived and taken the two bodies away, just as if it had been a normal car crash.'

The woman sat down next to her husband and remained silent for half a minute, which was no mean achievement for her. Then she nodded knowingly as if she had been aware all along that there was something mysterious and sinister about the accident.

'We all agreed there was something strange about it,' she said. 'Frau Doerrer at the bakery said that the driver must have fallen asleep at the wheel to crash into a tree at that time of the morning with no traffic on the roads. And the car was so distorted you could hardly tell the back from the front.'

'Don't you go wagging your tongue woman,' remonstrated the man, resuming his eating. 'We don't want the police round here asking questions.'

'Bah,' sneered the woman going back to her stove. 'You think I'd gossip? It's more than your life's worth nowadays.'

* * *

Klaire was wiping his forehead with a damp sponge. Her hand smelled of eau-de-cologne. Painfully, he moved his arm and took hold of her hand intending to kiss it, but he encountered some resistance.

'Hello, Mr Leigh. Glad to see you're back in the land of the living,' said a voice, pleasant and young, but not Klaire's.

Slowly, apprehensively, Simon Leigh opened his eyes. At first they did not focus very well, and the light hurt abominably like with a bad hangover but worse. But gradually, if he did not keep them open for too long at a time, he could make things out.

He was in a small room, furnished with the bed in which he lay, two chairs and a wash-basin. On the far wall was hung a poor Monet reproduction. The room was painted white — it was impersonal, spotlessly clean and had that unmistakable hospital smell about it. By his side was a high table with a telephone on it.

He turned his attention from the room, to the owner of the voice, which in his drugged subconscious, he had mistaken for Klaire's.

She was young, no more than twenty. Her ash blonde hair was cut short and she was wearing the starched uniform of a nurse. She smiled down at him. Her face matched her voice — pretty and warm. As his eyes focused better, he saw that she had dimples at the corners of her mouth. She was altogether very appealing.

The nurse picked up the telephone from the bed-side table.

'Doctor,' she said, 'Mr Leigh has regained consciousness.'

She replaced the receiver and felt Leigh's pulse.

'The doctor will be along to have a look at you in a few minutes. How do you feel?'

'I don't know yet.' He smiled weakly, although it hurt him to speak. 'Be a good girl and tell me where I am and what happened.'

'You are in St George's Hospital, Hyde Park Corner,' she said, straightening his bedclothes and fluffing out his pillows. 'I understand you were involved in a car accident in Germany. Now lie still and don't try to speak.'

'How did I get here?' asked Leigh.

'They had you flown here. You've been badly concussed and this is the first time you've regained consciousness in the three days since you've been here.'

She forestalled Leigh's next question.

'Today is Sunday, the 8th May.' She looked at her watch and smiled at him. '4.30 p.m. Right, no more talking. The Information Bureau has shut down until the doctor arrives!'

Leigh tried to match her smile, but his mouth hurt too much. He wondered what he looked like. From the way he felt, pretty ghastly he guessed. He thought it time to try and explore the extent of his injuries. He wiggled both his feet successfully. So far, so good. When he tried to sit up, there was an agonizing pain across his back and he flopped back on to the bed exhausted.

'What are you trying to do, Mr Leigh?' the nurse remonstrated sternly. 'Lie quiet until the doctor comes. I don't want to have to speak to you again.'

Simon Leigh closed his eyes and tried to think back to the accident, but try as he might he could not remember being in a car crash or even being in Germany. The only scene that came to his mind was that of a dark room, a nightclub perhaps. There was a bright blue spotlight, and there was a girl on the stage. A girl with long, black hair, tall and very beautiful. She was wearing a white evening gown and was undressing on the stage.

Leigh screwed up his eyes tightly, feverishly trying to remember, but just as he thought he was getting somewhere the door opened, and his concentration was broken.

A young coloured doctor, with friendly eyes and a good-natured face, came over to the bed and stood smiling down at him.

'Well, you've certainly been in the wars, haven't you, Mr Leigh? How do you feel?' he asked, in the rich melodious voice of a West Indian.

'I've been trying to find out, doctor,' Leigh replied, the effort of speaking hurting less.

'Well, lie still while I examine you.'

The nurse stood next to the doctor, while the latter examined Leigh's head, stomach, back and arms. Leigh watched his face closely trying to read something there, but by no change of expression did the doctor let him know how scarred his body was, or how inflamed and bruised his face.

'Well,' said the doctor at last replacing his stethoscope around his neck and tapping Leigh's knees with the side of his hand to test the reflexes. 'I'm afraid you'll live!'

'Doctor,' said Leigh, realizing for the first time, how shaky his voice sounded. 'Tell me honestly what is the matter with me.'

The doctor sat down on the chair next to the bed.

'Thank you nurse, that will be all.'

Dimples, as Leigh had christened the nurse left the room with a quick smile of reassurance.

'As you probably remember, Mr Leigh, you were involved in a bad road accident in Germany. You were lucky to escape with your life.'

The doctor, who did not yet know how much Leigh remembered did not want to mention the girl found dead in the car beside him.

'You have suffered a serious concussion and there is severe bruising and lacerations on your back next to the kidney and on your chest, stomach and arms. Your face and head have also suffered to some extent. However, there is nothing broken or permanently damaged, although some of the scars on your body may never completely heal. Believe me, Mr Leigh, you're a very lucky man to be alive today. It must have been quite an accident.'

'That's the strange part, doctor,' said Leigh, slowly. 'I can't remember the car crash or Germany or anything.'

'Nothing to worry about, I assure you,' said the doctor. 'This temporary amnesia is a result of the concussion. You'll find in a few days that everything will come back to you, clear as a bell.'

Leigh looked at the doctor. He could tell that he was not lying. A thought struck him.

'Tell me, doctor, who had me brought

here and told you who I was and what had happened?'

'A Mr Gorebain, from the Admiralty, I believe, took care of everything. He came with you in the ambulance from the airport, said he was a friend of yours.'

At the mention of Gorebain's name, some fragments of memory momentarily returned to Leigh. He had a fleeting image of a bar, and a short man with a flabby face and cold eyes: the man was smoking a cigar, a big cigar. There was something strange about the cigar but his mind blurred and the scene disappeared.

Then the image of a nightclub reappeared but again he could get no further; he did not try. He let his mind go blank — his head ached with the effort of trying to remember. 'Christ it hurt.'

Quietly the doctor left the room. On the way back to his office he had a few words with the nurse.

Simon Leigh made no attempt to fight the sleep that immediately invaded his confused mind. It was not a restful sleep, he tossed and turned continually and woke up screaming some hours later. It was night and there was only one small light on in the room. The nightnurse who had heard his screams came running into the room.

'I'm sorry, nurse,' he apologized. 'Just a nightmare.'

He lay back while the nurse wiped his face with a flannel and adjusted the bedclothes.

'It must have been a bad one, Mr Leigh. Your pyjamas are saturated with perspiration.'

Leigh tried to smile.

The nurse was not nearly as attractive as Dimples, but she was pleasantly plump and maternal.

It had been a bad one. A tall man in a dark green military uniform was whipping him across the face with a leather belt, whilst two large soldiers in leather coats, held him still, grinning with sadistic delight. The belt lashed him across the eyes, nose, ears, mouth. He could not move his face either way. He could not breathe or see. He was bleeding to death.

The nurse felt his pulse. 'I'll go and get you something to help you sleep. Lie quiet now.'

When the nurse returned, Leigh was lying motionless, drained of energy. She helped him to come to a sitting position and holding a glass of water in her hand, tried to put a small sleeping pill into his mouth.

He jerked himself painfully free from her and tried to speak. The words did not come easily.

'No-o. No, suicide pill. Don't want to die. Suki die.'

'What are you talking about, silly,' said the nurse patiently, as if speaking to a frightened child. 'This pill isn't going to make you die, it's to help you sleep.'

But nothing she could say or do would induce Leigh to take the sleeping pill. Finally she gave up and sat with him talking softly about silly, unimportant things until his incoherent ramblings ceased and he fell asleep.

She stayed for a while looking down at him and wondering. She looked beneath the scars and bruises, beneath the fear still showing on his face even in sleep.

She saw a cruel, cold face, good looking in a strange sort of way. Odd some of the injuries he had. You wouldn't think a car crash could inflict wounds in so many different parts of the body without causing serious damage in any one place.

What was it the doctor had said when they had brought him in from the ambulance that night?

'He looks more as if he's been savagely and scientifically beaten up than involved in a car accident.'

And who was this Suki. 'Suki die' he'd kept repeating when she was trying to get him to take the sleeping pill. Wasn't there something about a girl with long black hair who had been found dead next to him in the car. That must be Suki. Probably his wife. Poor devil, wonder how long it will be before he remembers. So often the delayed shock is the worst part of these temporary amnesia cases. Oh well, he'll be all right till morning.

She tucked in the bed and pushing his damp hair off his forehead went back to her office to write up her report.

12

To Sleep Perchance to Dream

When Peter Gorebain had finished speaking to the doctor on the phone he asked his Secretary to get Harold Levenson on the line for him.

While he was waiting for the call to come through he thought back to the strange cable that had arrived from East Berlin via the Russian Ambassador in London. It had been addressed to the Foreign Office but was quickly passed on by them to the Secret Service.

'Who the devil was the woman found dead in the car with Simon Leigh?' Perhaps now Simon had regained consciousness, the whole thing could be cleared up. The doctor had said that his memory should return in full in a day or two, he was already beginning to remember things.

Gorebain had a copy of the cable in his

desk. He unlocked the drawer and laying the flimsy sheet of copy paper on the desk studied it for the hundredth time, trying to read something between the lines. Trying to read a message that was possibly not even contained there.

It read —

FROM: THE MINISTRY OF TRADE, EAST BERLIN, FEDERAL REPUBLIC OF EAST GERMANY.

'TO: HIS EXCELLENCY, THE SOVIET AMBASSADOR, LONDON, ENGLAND.

FOR THE ATTENTION OF : THE FOREIGN OFFICE LONDON ENGLAND.

REGRET TO ADVISE U.K. CITIZEN, SIMON LEIGH, PASSPORT NO. 827342, BADLY HURT IN ROAD ACCIDENT STOP AT PRESENT UNDERGOING TREATMENT EAST BERLIN STATE HOSPITAL STOP RETURNING AEROFLOT FLIGHT 297 ARRIVING LONDON HEATHROW 16.40 HOURS SUNDAY 6TH MAY STOP WOMAN FOUND IN

CAR WITH LEIGH DEAD STOP PLEASE CONFIRM RECEIPT STOP.'

Seldom were the officially non-existent diplomatic channels between London and East Berlin utilized, but Levenson had immediately instructed the Foreign Office and more directly the Foreign Secretary, to send a cable to the Ministry of Trade, East Berlin via His Excellency, The Soviet Ambassador in London, thanking the East Germans for their trouble and confirming that an ambulance would be at Heathrow to meet Leigh's plane on arrival.

★　★　★

Sunday, 6th May, had started life as a sunny, late spring day. Towards midday however, a violent thunderstorm had erupted, and at four o'clock the rain was still bucketing down.

Peter Gorebain, waiting on the steps of his elegant Eaton Square flat for his chauffeur, cursed for having left his umbrella at the Admiralty.

After ten miserable minutes he was debating whether to go back into his flat to find out what had happened to his chauffeur when the black car came round the corner from Elizabeth Street, and pulled up at the steps.

The chauffeur jumped out and opened the car door.

'Sorry I'm late, sir. Battery trouble. Car wouldn't start.'

'That's all right, John,' said Gorebain, thankful of the warmth of the heater, as he settled himself in the back of the car. 'Take me to London Airport, will you, and make it snappy. The plane I am meeting lands in half an hour.'

'Right you are, sir,' said the chauffeur cheerfully, giving his terrifying imitation of a Humber Hawk doing a racing start at Le Mans.

'John,' said Gorebain drily. 'I would prefer to arrive at the Airport in one piece, if it's all the same to you.'

Resentfully John slowed the car down to a steady forty along the Cromwell Road.

They had arrived at the Airport with

ten minutes to spare before the scheduled arrival time of Leigh's flight but the plane had been forty minutes late landing and Gorebain after sending the car back to London, had paced nervously up and down the wet observation platform. He was dreading finding out how badly hurt Simon Leigh really was and when the Ilyushin jet landed he had ridden out in the waiting ambulance to the boarding steps.

The rain had relented to a steady drizzle and Gorebain had waited apprehensively at the foot of the steps until all the passengers had disembarked.

Then a stretcher carried by two members of the Russian crew was slowly brought down the steps.

To all intents and purposes the body lying motionless on the stretcher was dead. It took a few moments for Gorebain to positively identify it as Simon Leigh.

The head was completely bandaged and the usually tanned face was deathly white in between the patches of raw red skin. A deep scarlet gash stretched across the upper lip and the body was a mass of bruises, abrasions and lacerations.

Gorebain had instructed the ambulance driver and his assistant to take Leigh's suitcase and briefcase into the ambulance and immediately they had sped off, siren ringing and lights flashing towards London, where Gorebain had arranged a private room in St George's Hospital.

The doctor, who had come in the ambulance, had started to examine Leigh immediately, but after shining a pencil torch into the glazed eyes, he had stopped.

'Sorry, can't do anything for him now. He's in a comatose state — been heavily drugged. Daren't touch him until we get him to hospital. Some of these injuries look far worse than they are though,' he had added, catching sight of Gorebain's expression and pale face.

'I hope to God you're right,' Gorebain had whispered under his breath, sickened by the deathly figure of his friend lying apparently lifeless on the stretcher in front of him.

Thank God the doctor had been right.

* * *

The harsh ringing of the telephone brought Gorebain's thoughts away from the ambulance and back to the present.

He picked up the receiver. 'Gorebain.'

'Your call to Mr Levenson, sir.' Gorebain put the copy of the cable back into the desk drawer and locked it.

'Hello, Harold. I've just spoken to the hospital. Simon Leigh is still suffering from partial amnesia. He does not yet remember everything that took place. The doctor thinks his memory will return completely within a week or so.'

'How is he otherwise?' asked Levenson, lighting a big cigar.

'Fair. The doctor said there should be no permanent damage although he's been pretty badly knocked about one way and another.'

'I can imagine,' said Levenson drily. 'Have you found out who the girl was and how she figures in this whole business?'

'No, Harold. I don't think we'll know that until Simon regains his memory completely and we've had a chance to talk to him.'

'All right, Peter. Nothing more we can do at the moment. When can we visit him?'

'Not before Wednesday, the doctor said.'

'O.K. Wednesday it is. Keep me informed of any change in his condition. Oh Peter, before you go, the Lab boys keep asking if their little cigar invention was successful and as you're more directly concerned with that side of things than I am, perhaps you'll have a word with them next time you're in the building.'

'Yes, of course, Harold. Goodbye.'

Gorebain sat back, his brow furrowed with worry. He lit a cigarette and watched the smoke spiral to the ceiling, thicken for a moment and then disappear.

After this would Simon ever trust him again. Sometimes it was very difficult to put duty before friendship. Gorebain had often been sickened by the things he had to do — or ask other men to do — in the line of duty, but for the first time he was genuinely saddened as well.

The telephone once again brought an abrupt halt to Gorebain's uncharacteristic daydreaming.

'Gorebain.'

'Mr Levenson for you again, sir,' said his secretary.

'Hello, Peter. It struck me that you might like to talk to Leigh on your own first. I can always see him with you later.'

'Well, Harold, if you wouldn't mind, I think perhaps it would be better.'

'O.K. Let me know when you've seen him. Bye again.'

'It's funny,' thought Gorebain, 'how Levenson usually utterly ruthless and insensitive can on occasion be understanding, even considerate. Must be getting sentimental like me,' he thought with a wry smile.

Levenson was not becoming sentimental, but he was at the moment very worried. There were few men in the Western World, and certainly no other man in England who had so much experience and knowledge of the workings of the minds of the Communists as

Harold Levenson. Usually the Russians and their satellites behaved, to say the least, unpredictably, but even so, through past experience and informed guessing, Levenson could and generally did come up with the right answers.

But in the present situation, he was absolutely mystified. He had not slept properly for a week trying to see a ray of light at the end of the wood — but it was no good, the more he thought about it, the less he understood. He was repeatedly forced to return to one crucial surmise.

'Why had the East Germans set Simon Leigh free?' He knew from the intelligence report he had received soon after the General's death, that Leigh had been taken in for questioning. So far, so good. 'But why then hadn't they either released him as innocent or kept him if they suspected or knew him to be guilty.'

Levenson was too shrewd to believe the story of the car crash. It was possible, of course, but somehow through no explanation that he could have put into words, he knew there was a lot more to it than that. If Leigh had been found guilty, or even if they merely suspected him, why go to all the trouble of the car crash.

And then taking it one step further, if for some unknown reason, they had decided to stage a car crash to dispose of Leigh, why then go to all the trouble of keeping him alive and having him flown back to England. Why not just kill him and have done with it — no one could prove that he had not died in the car crash.'

There was some simple key to the whole affair: of that Levenson was convinced. He was equally convinced the key was contained, unknowingly perhaps, in Simon Leigh's brain.

⋆ ⋆ ⋆

There was logic in Harold Levenson's reasoning, and no doubt under normal circumstances Leigh would have been killed outright, but the circumstances at four o'clock that fateful morning in the small first floor office in East Berlin had been far from normal.

Colonel Muller was livid that he had

been cheated of his confession when he had been so very near. He knew that another few minutes with the soldiers working on the girl and Leigh would have signed anything; he would have had his treasured confession. How could he have foreseen that the girl would be concealing in her mouth the suicide capsule, assigned to all agents as a safe-guard against capture and interrogation by the other side. It was too ironical that she should have taken it to protect herself from her own 'employers'.

Now that Leigh was unconscious he knew he would never extract his confession in the time left to him. He would have to try and cover up as much as possible and perhaps with a little luck he could still take the General's place. He would have to be smart as well as lucky though. There was a lot to do.

'Get her out of here,' he had snapped at the two policemen, pointing distastefully to Suki's scarred body slumped lifeless in the chair, her arms and legs still bound tightly to prevent her moving.

The two policemen, who had thoroughly enjoyed the performance, looked at each other in perplexed silence.

'What shall we do with her, Herr Colonel?' one courageously asked at last.

'I don't care what you do with her. Just get her out of here,' Muller shouted fastening the blood stained belt back around his waist.

The two policemen who knew better than to fall foul of Colonel Muller's temper had quickly cut the ropes holding the body to the chair. Then taking hold of her wrists and feet they had half dragged, half carried the body out of the office leaving a trail of blood from the chair to the door.

Muller had a sudden idea and shouted after them.

'Clean her up as much as possible and come back here for her clothes. I'll tell you what to do then.'

The policemen left the room, muttering inaudible obscenities under their breath. They were paid, if you could call it pay, to be policemen, with special duties to the late General, not body washers to

Colonel Bloody Muller.

The Colonel picked up the phone and asked for a number. He was connected immediately.

'Hello, Comrade Ivanovitch, I'm sorry to trouble you again, but after a through investigation, I find Leigh to be innocent.'

'That is remarkably quick work. I gave you four hours and you have not used half that time.'

Ivanovitch, who was the permanent Russian Representative of the K.G.B. in East Berlin and had subsequent seniority over any of his East German colleagues hated loose ends: also he did not like or trust Muller. The man was too ambitious, too self-assured.

'My enquiries took less time than I had anticipated,' replied Muller, easily.

'Then who, Colonel,' Ivanovitch had asked in his deep voice, 'is guilty?'

'No one is guilty Comrade. The General did, in fact, die of a Coronary Thrombosis, caused probably by excessive eating and drinking at the banquet.' Muller added with a flash of inspiration.

'I see,' said Ivanovitch. 'In that case,

you'll have to release this Englishman, Leigh, now, won't you, I told you not to harm him in any way: I trust this order has not been disobeyed.'

'Of course not, Comrade. I'm sending him back to his hotel in my car at once.'

'Good. Apologize to him for any inconvenience and report back to me as soon as everything is satisfactorily settled and we can forget the whole tiresome affair.'

When the two policemen returned half an hour later later, Muller had collected his thoughts and was his normal relaxed self once again.

'I want you both to listen to me very carefully.'

He rose from his desk and came and stood in front of the two policemen, his bloodshot eyes threatening and dangerous.

'What has taken place tonight, here in this office, is to be forgotten immediately. Do you understand?'

'Yes, Herr Colonel,' they replied as one.

'If I ever find out that either of you have spoken to anyone, anyone at all about what you have seen, your lives won't be worth living.'

The two policemen, who did not doubt for one moment the sincerity of Colonel Muller's words had already forgotten everything that they had witnessed and taken part in.

Muller pointed to Suki's torn and rumpled clothes lying in a heap on the floor.

'I want you,' he continued, 'to take these clothes and dress the girl in them so that she looks as she did when she came in.'

He ignored the looks of incredulity on the two men's faces.

'Then you are to take my car and crash it; crash it badly and convincingly somewhere between here and Leigh's hotel. You are to place this man,' he gestured towards Leigh, still unconscious in the chair, 'in the driver's seat and the girl's body next to him in the front seat of the wreckage.

'But,' he paused to let his words sink in, 'wait until immediately after the crash before you do this. Do you understand?

This man is not to be injured any more. It must appear as if he has simply been involved in a car accident. You may enlist the help of two comrades and take a truck. Is this all clear to you?'

'Ja, Herr Colonel.'

When the Colonel had reported to Ivanovitch some hours later, he felt satisfied that he had left nothing to chance.

'Comrade Ivanovitch, I have some distressing news to report.'

There was an unnerving silence at the other end of the line.

'It is this Leigh again,' Muller continued quickly. 'I sent him back to his hotel in my car and he had an accident on the way. I understand he hit a tree. The events of the past few hours, plus the drink he had consumed at the banquet must have had more effect on him than I had realized.'

'Your little dinner tonight seems to have caused no end of trouble,' said Ivanovitch icily. 'First it is blamed for the General's heart attack and now for this car accident. Why was Leigh driving anyway?'

'I had sent my driver home. I did not want to keep him hanging around all night,' Muller replied without hesitation.

'Is Leigh dead?'

'No, Comrade. He's in a bad way, but the doctors think that he'll live.'

'Leigh was alone, of course, when he crashed the car?'

'No, that's the funny part. With him in the car was the Agent who had been assigned to him in Brussels. She was in East Berlin at the General's instructions. She must have somehow contacted Leigh. She was killed outright.'

'You seem once again, Colonel Muller, to have found out a great deal in a remarkably short space of time,' said Ivanovitch.

Muller wondered if this was intended as a compliment; somehow he doubted it.

'This Agent was at the dinner?'

'No, Comrade Ivanovitch, the General did not want Leigh to know who she really was. It was his intention that they should not meet. Leigh was returning to London on Friday anyway.'

There was a momentary pause. 'Wait

until you hear from me,' said Ivanovitch, replacing the receiver.

He was far from convinced by Colonel Muller's story. The man was too glib, too quick with his answers.

He summoned his immediate subordinate.

'Yuri, this incident with the General's death and Leigh and so on is getting out of hand. Muller tells me that Leigh has had a car crash and is badly hurt and that the girl who was assigned to watch him in Brussels has been killed. Somehow the whole thing does not tie up. I want the truth from Muller. Have him brought here and find out what really happened, by the usual methods if he proves unco-operative. He's too ambitious to be of any further service to us.'

Yuri, who had been an instructor in interrogation techniques at one of the three spy-schools in Moscow, was an expert at the art of extracting information. He left the room smiling to himself. His talents had lain dormant for too long. It would not do to grow stale.

Ivanovitch picked up the telephone.

'Get Colonel Muller back on the line for me.'

The overworked night switchboard operator at the Ministry of Trade put the call through to Muller's office.

What a night this had been. The phones had not stopped ringing for one minute. She would not be sorry when her relief came on duty at eight o'clock and she could go home and get some sleep.

'I have a call for you, Colonel, hold the line, please,' she said automatically.

Ivanovitch's voice was friendlier than before and Muller was reassured. He, who should have known better.

'Colonel Muller, exactly how badly hurt is Leigh?'

'The doctors say he won't die, but he is badly concussed and bruised.'

'I see,' Ivanovitch thought quickly. There could be serious international repercussions if this situation was mishandled any more than it already had been.

'Colonel, I would like you to send a cable immediately, via the normal channels from your Ministry to the Foreign

Office in London, explaining the situation and expressing regret. Then I want Leigh flown back to England at our expense as soon as possible. The man has caused nothing but trouble ever since he's been here. Oh, and Colonel, stay in your office. I'm sending someone over to see you about something.'

Colonel Muller replaced the receiver and smiled smugly to himself. He thought that Ivanovitch had sounded pleased with the way he had handled things and he waited expectantly for his visitor, sure that he was about to be informed of his forthcoming promotion. He, too, was exhausted and drained of energy, but for this news he would have willingly climbed a mountain.

'I must do something about clearing up this room though,' he thought, catching sight of the bloodstains spattered across the floor. 'Even though I'll soon be moving upstairs.'

Then a sudden thought struck him. Why should Leigh go free after all the trouble and harm he had caused. If he could· prove which he had no doubt he could given time — that Leigh had murdered the General, then surely the end would justify the means even to Ivanovitch. If Muller presented him with a fait accompli, the Russian could only congratulate him. Anyway as the General's successor he could virtually make his own decisions.

He picked up the telephone and put a private call through to his flat which he shared with his younger brother, who had also worked for the General. Muller would have trusted Heinrich with his life. They had always been close and had followed the same career since being in the Hitler Youth together. Heinrich idolized his elder brother and would have cut off his right arm for him if necessary.

'Hello, Heinrich,' said Muller, when his brother's sleepy voice answered the telephone. 'I'm sorry to wake you up, but I must see you at once.'

'What is it Adolf?' Heinrich asked immediately alert.

When he had replaced the receiver, Heinrich immediately began to dress. He closely resembled his brother although he was shorter and also he had lost all his hair at a very early age and was completely bald.

★ ★ ★

Simon Leigh slept a lot during the next few days. His treatment was progressing well and consisted mainly of plenty of rest and sleep. The doctor assured him that nature would heal all his injuries in time. The only place where an operation had been necessary was on his upper lip, which had been split open by Muller's metal watch strap.

Each time he awoke he remembered a little more of what had taken place in Brussels and East Berlin. The pieces of the jigsaw were gradually fitting together in his mind, with the exception of the car crash and his return to England. Try as he might, he could not recall any details of his accident in East Berlin or anything that had happened subsequent to it until he woke up in St George's Hospital. He was assured by the doctor that this amnesia would disappear completely in time.

One cold evening at six o'clock, a black Admiralty Humber Hawk skilfully negotiated the rush hour traffic at Hyde Park Corner and dropped Peter Gorebain off on the steps of St George's Hospital.

' 'Night, sir,' called the chauffeur.

'Good night, John.'

Gorebain had telephoned in the afternoon to say he was coming, and 'Dimples' was in Leigh's room busily straightening the bedclothes.

'It'll be nice for you to have a visitor, won't it?'

Leigh had developed a special affection for this nurse and he playfully squeezed her hand. This time she made no move to take it away.

'As soon as I'm allowed to shave,' he said, 'I'm going to give you a great big kiss. If I tried now, I'd scratch your face with my beard.'

'In that case,' said the nurse laughing, 'I think a beard definitely suits you.'

There was a knock on the door and Gorebain, correct as ever in a dark grey three piece suit and stiff white collared shirt entered the room smiling a little nervously.

The nurse after a word of greeting to Gorebain, whom she had met briefly when they had brought Leigh in from the ambulance left the room.

'Hello, Simon. How are you feeling?' Gorebain came forward and took the chair at the side of the bed. 'You certainly look a darned sight better than the last time I saw you.'

'I should imagine a ghost would have looked better than that,' Leigh replied.

He had often thought of what he would say to Gorebain when they met; he knew that the man had only been doing his duty and it would not be fair to blame or hold him responsible for what had happened.

Leigh smiled slowly. 'Hello, Peter. Good to see you again.'

Outwardly Gorebain showed no emotion, but inwardly his heart lifted with joy.

'Simon,' he said, 'now is not the time to discuss things in any great detail, but I do want you to know that we're proud of you. What you did, apart from saving many lives, prevented priceless information being acquired by the East Germans and, of course, the Russians.'

Leigh said nothing. He wanted to forget that side of his trip. He wanted to ask Gorebain the question which had been troubling him since he had first regained consciousness.

'Peter, what's this about a car crash?'

'I was hoping you'd be able to tell me about that,' replied Gorebain in a puzzled voice. 'You mean you don't remember it?'

'Not a thing.'

'The Ministry of Trade in East Berlin cabled us that you had been involved in a bad car accident and that they were having you flown back to London. They said that the girl found in the wreckage of the car beside you was dead.'

Leigh lay back and closed his eyes. 'So that was it, the bastards. What a diabolical scheme. Muller was certainly an able candidate for the General's successor.'

'Simon,' Gorebain continued, 'who was this girl?'

Leigh did not answer immediately, then

he opened his eyes and looked at Peter Gorebain.

'Her name was Suki Laval,' he said wearily. 'I was going to ask her to marry me.'

Now it was Gorebain's turn to be speechless. When he did speak, his voice was gentle. 'Do you want to talk about it, Simon?'

'Peter, just now you said this wasn't the right time to go into details and quite honestly I don't feel up to it. In a day or two I'll tell you anything you want to know, but I really am very tired. Before you go, I want you to do something for me.'

'Of course. What is it?'

Painfully Leigh propped himself up on one elbow. When he spoke his voice held a note of urgency as if he was afraid his strength would give out before he had finished.

'This girl, Suki Laval. She was working for the Communists. We met in Brussels and she was assigned to file a full report on me there, although I didn't find that out till later,' he added bitterly.

234

Gorebain sat up straight in his chair. 'They must have suspected you then, before you even arrived in East Berlin.'

'No, they didn't suspect a thing. As Levenson kept drumming into me, they're just naturally thoroughly suspicious people. I want you, Peter, to find out absolutely everything you can about this girl, Suki Laval. How long she had been working for them, how she was recruited, in fact anything and everything. I can give you a little information to go on but the rest is up to you.'

'I can't promise anything, Simon,' said Gorebain. 'But I'll certainly do my best for you.'

He took from his breast pocket, a small leather notebook and a slim pen. 'O.K., fire away.'

Leigh took a deep breath and willed himself to remember everything. He was still weak and the doctor had ordered him to keep conversation with Gorebain to a minimum. He closed his eyes again and, trying to keep the facts in the right order, told Gorebain everything he knew about the girl. Everything she had ever told him and some things which she had not. When he had finished more than half an hour later, he was exhausted and lay back in the bed as if asleep.

Gorebain, who had covered many pages of his notebook in his small precise handwriting, looked at Leigh.

'She must have meant a lot to you, Simon.'

'She did, Peter,' said Leigh, not opening his eyes. 'It's been wonderful seeing you again, but I really am terribly tired now. I'm not used to talking so much.'

Leigh was asleep before Gorebain had left the room.

★ ★ ★

Ten days later, Simon Leigh left hospital. He was still not one hundred per cent fit but he could not tolerate the boredom of lying in bed, doing nothing any longer.

The doctor had resignedly given in to his request to be discharged, but had warned him to take things easy for a while.

Although his face was almost completely healed, he had been advised not to begin shaving for another fortnight.

Dimples helped him to pack and when he was ready to leave, she held out her hand to him.

'Goodbye, Simon. God bless you.'

He took her hand and pulled her into his arms. She did not resist. Then he kissed her on the lips as gently as his beard would permit.

She tried to pretend that she was not crying.

'You told me a beard suited me, so you'll have to suffer the consequences of it,' he told her, kissing her again.

Leigh had arranged with the garage which had kept and serviced his car while he was away, to send a driver to pick him up from St George's Hospital.

As he swung himself into the Bristol's unfamiliar passenger seat, Simon Leigh realized for the first time how happy he was to be alive — despite everything. How wonderful to be able to drive this superbly made car at high speed again: to get unashamedly drunk in some quiet bar: to win a shattering game of squash and cool off in the unheated swimming pool at his Club.

He understood for the first time in his life, the popular belief that one does not really appreciate life until one has been very near to death.

He sat back in the rich leather upholstery of the Bristol and sighed. It was a sigh of both relief and regret.

13

The Bitter Pill of Truth

Eighteen months before his trip to East Berlin, Simon Leigh had applied to the Postmaster General for permission to have a telephone installed in his car.

He had received a polite letter back informing him that out of several thousand annual applications for private car telephones, only a set quota of permits were issued to private individuals, and as this quota currently fell far below the demand, while Leigh's application would be registered it might be some time before a permit was granted to him.

Leigh was, therefore, delighted to find on leaving hospital that amongst the mail awaiting him at his flat was an official authorization from the G.P.O. for him to effect the installation of a telephone in his car, subject to the usual charges and conditions.

The telephone was installed one Thursday and early the following morning while he was driving to his office, he received his first call on it. The unfamiliar ringing of the phone cleverly fixed beneath the dashboard shattered Leigh's thoughts of production problems and price structures, and he reached forward to lift the receiver off its cradle.

'Leigh.'

'Hello, Simon. Peter Gorebain here. Sorry to have to phone you so early, but I wanted to catch you before you left your flat.'

Leigh braked sharply at some traffic lights, which had just changed to red.

'I'm not in my flat, Peter. I'm on my way to the office.'

He explained to Gorebain that he had arranged for the phone number of his flat to be interchangeable with that of the car, so that at the flick of a master switch on his car telephone the line was automatically transferred to his flat and vice versa.

Gorebain gave a chuckle. 'You're becoming a type-cast millionaire, Simon. It'll be a chauffeur driven Rolls Royce with tinted windows next.'

As Leigh pulled away from the lights, he was amused by the incredulous look on the face of an elderly lady, sitting in a bus which had pulled up alongside the Bristol: her mouth was half-open as if she could not believe even in this day and age that a man could actually sit in his car and conduct a telephone conversation.

'No Peter, not for a few years yet. I'll leave chauffeur driven cars to you Civil Servants.'

Gorebain laughed again, then he became serious. 'The reason I'm phoning you, Simon, is that I think we've got the information you're after. Could you possibly meet me for lunch today?'

Leigh, who had a frantically busy day ahead of him, and could ill afford the time answered immediately.

'Yes, Peter, I'll have lunch with you. Where and when?'

'Say Le Coq d'Or, at one-thirty.'

'I'll be there, Peter. Goodbye and thank you.'

★ ★ ★

241

As Leigh brought the Bristol out on to the M.4 he thought back to the last time he had seen Peter Gorebain. It was a few days before he had left hospital and he had been lying in bed one afternoon, thoroughly fed up and depressed with the boredom of doing nothing day after day, when Dimples had come into the room and announced that Mr Harold Levenson and Mr Peter Gorebain were outside.

Levenson had entered the room first and with a lecherous wink at the departing Dimples, had come over to one of the bedside chairs and sat down with a sigh of relief, as if he had been afraid that he might have to stand.

Gorebain, with a brief greeting to Leigh had taken the chair on the opposite side of the bed and Leigh had waited for Levenson to begin speaking.

'Well, Simon, how are you?' he had asked at last, when he sensed that Gorebain was about to speak.

'I'm in the pink of health,' Leigh replied, but his sarcasm appeared to be wasted on the Head of the British Secret Service.

Levenson leaned forward and rested his elbows on the bed.

'Simon,' he said, 'I want you to know that your mission was a complete success. Not only from the point of view of disposing of the General who was, to say the least, a danger to British Security at home and abroad, but equally important it saved the lives and working capacity of all our field agents in East Germany. I was speaking to the Foreign Secretary yesterday and he asked me to convey to you his sincerest personal congratulations. Unofficially, of course.'

Leigh wondered if Levenson expected him to thank him for the message. If he did he was going to be disappointed.

He had lain back in the bed and waited for Levenson to come to the reason for his visit. It did not take long.

After eating a couple of grapes from the bowl by Leigh's bed, Levenson had cleared his throat and wiped some imaginary beads of perspiration from his broad brow.

'Simon,' he said, 'I know you're not still fully recovered from your 'accident' but it would assist us a great deal, if you could give a full account of everything that happened to you in East Berlin from start to finish. Take your time and try not to leave anything out. It really is vitally important.'

Leigh had known that sooner or later he would have to re-live a period of his life he desperately wanted to forget. Closing his eyes with the effort of trying to keep his facts in the right order he had told them everything that had happened to him, starting with Suki in Brussels and ending with the last thing he remembered — Muller beating him across the head and face while he was tied to the chair.

Levenson and Gorebain had both listened in silence to everything he said their faces expressionless, Gorebain making the occasional note.

When he had finished Leigh asked Levenson a question.

'Tell me, Harold, the waiter in the Hotel Mannheim, who is he?'

'He's one of our plants,' Levenson had replied briefly.

The only thing that Leigh could not tell

them about was the car crash. He had been unconscious the whole time and had no recollection of it.

'It's not really important, Simon,' Levenson had said. 'The whole thing was obviously a put-up job. They could not send you back to England, innocent as they supposed you to be, in the state you were in without providing some sort of explanation. The girl Laval was already dead, so they had a convenient way of killing two birds with one stone, so to speak. Also, as you were unconscious you could hardly prove that you were not in a car crash. Quite ingenious in its way.'

They had talked of other things for some time and then Levenson had stood up to go. At the door he had paused and looked back.

'She must have been a brave girl, Simon. By God, you're damned lucky to be alive.'

'No thanks to you.' Leigh remembered thinking at the time.

Gorbain had stayed behind after Levenson had gone and Leigh had asked him the question, which was he hoped going to be answered today.

'Any news for me yet about Suki Laval, Peter?'

Gorebain had shaken his head. 'These things take time, Simon, but you can rest assured that if the information is obtainable, we'll get it.'

Leigh had nodded trying to keep his disappointment from showing.

'I only hope to God that the information is worth waiting so long for,' Leigh thought as he brought his mind back to the present. He swung the Bristol through the Factory gates, returning the salute of one of his engineers who was marching briskly across the yard.

So much work had accumulated in his absence that Leigh found himself working all hours of the day and night again, like at the beginning. He felt perfectly fit now and apart from the scars on his body, appeared to have suffered no permanent ill-effects from the car crash, which was the officially circulated reason for his injuries.

He had made Donald Joyce a Director of the Company and was having talks with a merchant back in the city about the possibility of going Public. Business had never been better and Leigh was thinking of building an additional factory in nearby Slough, if he could obtain Planning Permission for the site he had his eye on.

Although he was working at pressure, a day did not pass when Leigh's thoughts did not turn at some time to Suki Laval. His visit to East Berlin was, despite the initial amnesia he had suffered, as fresh and vivid as if it had been yesterday. But somehow as time passed, although losing nothing of its reality, the whole episode became slightly glazed in his mind, as if it was something he was very familiar with, more through having read about it, than through actually having experienced himself.

Leigh was not looking forward to his lunch with Gorebain. It was like going to a doctor whom you are afraid might tell you that you have an incurable disease. On the other hand he might tell you there is nothing wrong with you, but still you are wary of setting foot in the surgery.

Had Suki's words meant anything, when she had first entered Colonel Muller's office that fateful night? Or had they been just words.

'I'm so sorry, *chéri*,' she had said, cradling his body in her arms. 'Some day you will understand and perhaps forgive. Do not hate me.'

Leigh was frightened of discovering the truth and it was with apprehension that he rose from his desk at one o'clock. With a quick word to Janine, his secretary, that he would be back later in the day, he left his office.

* * *

Le Coq d'Or was as busy as it is every lunchtime. Gorebain was sitting at his usual window table, overlooking Stratton Street. He watched the chauffeur-driven Bentleys and Daimlers purr to the door and disgorge their sleek, well fed looking occupants.

A few minutes after one-thirty, he saw Leigh's silver grey Bristol draw impressively to the door. 'Some cars look powerful but aren't, but there's no hypocrisy about that one,' he thought admiringly, as Simon stepped out of the car and handed the keys to the doorman.

Leigh looked much better than the last time Gorebain had seen him. His hair which had been shaved to treat the injuries to his head, had grown to its normal length. His lean face, now clean shaven had regained some of its usual colour and bore only one faint scar on the upper lip where the stitches had been removed.

Gorebain knew that underneath the Savile Row suit and handmade pale blue shirt, there would be more souvenirs of Leigh's business trip to Communist Berlin, but the doctor had said that most of those scars should fade even disappear in time.

Leigh glanced at his watch as he entered the Restaurant. Twenty to two.

He stood in the doorway of the Restaurant for a minute looking round, then he spotted Gorebain at his window table and walked over.

The two men shook hands warmly.

'Sorry, I'm a bit late, Peter. The traffic was impossible from Knightsbridge.'

'That's all right. What are you drinking, Simon? The bar was so crowded that I thought it better for us to have a drink in here before eating.'

'I'll have a lager. I'm working this afternoon and this breathalyser business scares the life out of me.'

'Simon,' said Gorebain seriously. 'I don't think you will be working this afternoon. Harold Levenson asked me to take you along to his office after lunch. He told me not to tell you anything before you saw him. Sorry to have to keep you in suspense, but it won't be for much longer now. Perhaps it would be as well if you phoned your office and told them that you won't be coming back today.'

Leigh nodded. 'I'll phone after we've eaten. Oh, and make that lager a Scotch. Double if you can afford it.' He smiled.

Over a superb lunch of Scotch Smoked Salmon, Venison pie and Camembert cheese, the two men talked of anything and everything except Suki.

Leigh tried to draw Gorebain to talk

about Harold Levenson. The man held a strange attraction or rather fascination for Leigh. Superficially he was so unlike the popular image of a Secret Service Chief that Leigh was intrigued to know what the man was really like inside. What made him tick. That he had a brilliant business brain everybody knew. That he was utterly ruthless and unscrupulous Leigh knew, but other than to make meaningless general comments, Gorebain would not discuss any personal details about Harold Levenson.

Finally, Leigh gave up and the conversation turned to yachts and sailing.

After the waiter had brought the coffee and brandy, Leigh relapsed into silence. He was tense and apprehensive at the thought of finally learning the truth about Suki Laval.

Gorebain who already knew the truth was glad that Levenson had not given him the job of telling Leigh.

When the bill was brought Leigh insisted on paying, despite Gorebain's protesting.

'I can put you down as a foreign buyer

from Peking and claim it back on expenses.' He smiled. Laughing, Gorebain had given in.

'Take me to thy leader,' Leigh said seriously as he started the Bristol's powerful engine.

Gorebain directed Leigh to Connaught Place and Leigh parked outside an elegant house on the right. It was the only detached house in the whole mews.

'Shall I lead the way, old boy?' said Gorebain, pushing open the heavy front door which was unlocked.

There was a metal plaque at the side of the door listing the names of several companies which were housed inside. They included a firm called 'Display Advertising Services Ltd.', with whom Leigh seemed to remember having once done some business, but he could not recall the details.

Inside, the house was like any business premises; smooth young men rushed about with files under their arms and worried expressions on their eager faces.

The building, which housed the Foreign and Administrative section of the

British Secret Service, contained the most powerful radio transmitter in Great Britain. The ground and upper floors of the building were genuinely concerned with legitimate business activities, although these were controlled by the Secret Service and more directly by Levenson. This explained why they all made embarrassingly large annual profits.

Gorebain nodded to the uniformed porter sitting importantly behind a large leather topped reception desk inside the doorway.

As they walked past the desk Leigh saw the man write something in a red book.

Gorebain led the way to a small automatic lift beside the main lift to the building. He pressed the button marked 'basement'.

Leigh thought it strange that they could not walk from street level to the basement.

As if reading his mind, Gorebain said, 'No stairs, old boy. This is the only way down.'

The two men emerged from the lift to

be faced with another uniformed porter sitting behind a desk directly opposite the lift doors. He, too, wrote in a red book as Leigh and Gorebain walked past him. Unknown to Leigh in the five minutes that he had been in the building his photograph had been taken three times by cameras concealed in the lift wall. Two profiles, one full face. Everyone that had ever used that lift had had their photograph taken and permanently filed. His fingerprints were about to be taken.

Gorebain led the way down a narrow passage starkly lit with naked light bulbs. The two mens' heels rang noisily on the stone floor.

'Hardly Levenson's style I would have thought,' said Leigh gesturing towards the bare walls and stone floor.

Gorebain smiled but made no reply. He did not tell Leigh that in a room on the other side of the wall was the world's most advanced X-ray machine — American, of course. Everyone that passed a certain point in the passage outside was 'vetted' by the machine to ensure that they were carrying no weapon or armament of any kind. If a weapon was suspected the machine immediately threw a metal screen across the passage, at the same time automatically locking the lift doors; thus whoever had been foolish enough to invade Harold Levenson's private sanctum carrying a weapon was trapped between the screen and the lift doors. The uniformed porter sitting behind the desk by the lift would immediately come to investigate. He was armed and would not hesitate to use his gun. Since the X-ray machine had been installed in 1965 only two people had been stopped by it. Both had been intending to kill the Head of the Secret Service, whose identity they did not know. Both themselves were now dead.

Gorebain led the way down the long passage to the last door on the left where he stopped. He pressed a buzzer on the outside of the door.

Harold Levenson sitting behind his desk on the other side of the door pressed a button on the arm of his chair. Immediately a special process in the heavy steel door, similar to the two-way mirror principle, framed a reflection of the two men waiting outside on the panel of the door.

He pressed a second switch which unlocked the three bullet proof locks.

Gorebain gestured for Leigh to precede him into the room.

Leigh put his hand on a highly polished brass door handle and turning it, pushed the heavy door open. He found himself in a large comfortable room, which in strong contrast to the stone floor of the corridor outside, was furnished in the manner of an expensive office, with thick Wilton carpet and tasteful contemporary furniture and fittings. The only thing that made it any different from a normal office was the complete absence of any natural light. Being in a basement there were, of course, no windows in the room. But the four sets of lights on the panelled walls gave out enough light for this to be not really noticeable.

Levenson rose from behind his desk and held out his podgy hand to Leigh.

After gesturing for Leigh to sit down, he turned his attention to Gorebain.

'Peter, I wonder if you would go along to the decoding room. There's some trouble with our weekly code word swop. Gregson tells me that the Chinese have cracked it three times during the last month. If that's correct, there must be a serious leak somewhere.'

Gorebain immediately left the room and Levenson pressed the button, re-locking the doors.

He sat back in his reclining chair.

'Cigar, Simon?'

'I'll smoke one of my own, if you don't mind.'

Levenson smiled. 'Don't trust my cigars eh?'

Leigh shrugged but did not return the smile.

The lighting in the room seemed to accentuate the flabbiness of Levenson's face. His mohair suit sparkled as if it was inset with diamonds.

Leigh wondered idly how much the man sitting opposite him was worth. Ten million, twenty? It was impossible to guess.

Both men spent some time going

through the cigar lighting ritual. When Levenson at last looked up his face was covered with perspiration although the office was air-conditioned.

'You already know, Simon,' he said, 'how very successful your mission to East Berlin was. I would like, now we're alone, to offer you my sincere personal congratulations and thanks.'

Leigh looked across the desk and narrowed his eyes.

'Harold, I don't want your congratulations or thanks. I want to wash my hands of the whole bloody business and forget it. You knew damned well that the chances of my leaving East Berlin alive were negligible. How I'm here now is a miracle. However, I didn't come here to pick a quarrel with you and I don't intend to. But before I can forget this business and you and everything connected with you, I have to know the truth about Suki Laval.'

Levenson looked at Leigh across the desk, his face expressionless. Then he nodded.

'Peter tells me that you were going to

marry this girl. Is that correct?'

'I was going to ask her to marry me, yes,' Leigh replied quietly.

Levenson puffed on his cigar.

'Simon,' he said, 'I've pulled every string, used every means at my disposal to get the answers for you. Believe me, it wasn't easy.'

From the little Leigh knew of Harold Levenson's sphere of influence, he knew those strings must have been considerable.

Levenson leaned forward and opened one of the desk drawers. He removed from it a blue cardboard folder, and half-reading, half from memory, began to speak.

'Miss Laval's father was French and her mother Hungarian.'

This much Leigh knew and he waited impatiently for Levenson to tell him what he really wanted to know.

'The Lavals lived in Paris for some time but in 1935 they moved to Budapest, where they opened a small bistro type restaurant.

'They ran the restaurant very successfully until the war came along. There is no record of what happened to them in the war years but the threads pick up again in 1950, which is when Suki, who had been born during the war comes into the picture.'

Leigh drew hard on his cigar, not tasting it.

'The Lavals,' Levenson continued, 'sent their young daughter to the Convent of the Sacred Heart in Brighton. The mother had some relatives who had emigrated here, and the education facilities in Hungary at that time were, to say the least, poor. They were determined to give their daughter the best schooling they could with the money they had saved before the war.

'They opened their restaurant again and it prospered as it had done previously. I understand that the father had a wonderful personality and was held in high esteem in Budapest.

'In 1956 when the Russians invaded Budapest and brutally crushed the uprising there, Suki Laval was at school over here and her mother wrote to the relatives asking if they could keep her in

England during the holidays until the trouble in Hungary sorted itself out as it must do one way or the other.'

Leigh closed his eyes and tried to picture a smiling schoolgirl in a gymslip, with a long black ponytail and clear grey eyes, as yet unsaddened by the cruel world in which she was living.

'One night,' Levenson went on, 'some Russian soldiers came to the restaurant for a meal. They were very drunk already. From what I can gather there was some dispute with the old man over the bill, which they either refused to pay or insisted on paying in Roubles, which were virtually valueless currency in Hungary.

'When the old man demanded payment in Hungarian florints they took it in turns to club him with their rifle butts, laughing and joking the whole time. The man was already old and weak and it did not take long for him to die.

'His wife, who had seen the argument brewing had rushed away to fetch help from the old man's friends, but when they returned to the restaurant, it was already too late. The soldiers had gone, leaving

Monsieur Laval lying dead on the floor in a pool of his own blood.'

Leigh gripped the arms of his chair tightly.

Levenson glanced up from the file, but Leigh gestured for him to continue.

'The old woman had a nervous breakdown and the daughter, who could not stay with the relatives in England indefinitely, returned home having been told only that her mother was not very well. The relatives had not had the courage to tell her about her father.

'When she arrived at the restaurant in Budapest, which was also her home, she found it closed up and shutters on all the windows. Apparently, she rushed to a girlfriend's house nearby and was told that her mother was in hospital.

'I'm sorry about your father,' the girlfriend had said. 'He was a good man.'

'What are you talking about. What's happened to my father,' Suki asked.

'When the surprised girl had told her what had happened, Suki did not break down. In fact, I understand from the girl, who was one of the people we had interviewed, that she thanked her quietly for her help and went straight to the hospital to see her mother.'

Again Levenson looked up from the folder. Leigh's face was expressionless and his eyes were fixed on the blank wall opposite him.

'Suki found her mother a changed woman. She was not young, but she had always been active and cheerful. Now she just lay in hospital, not speaking or moving. Suki had always been close to both her parents, but with her father she had shared a special relationship. Now she was determined to make up for his death to her mother, who had no one else to turn to.

'She did not return to school the following term. She had to work to keep herself and her mother. While at school she had spent all her free time taking dancing lessons, which she excelled at, but there was no call for straightforward dancing in Hungary at that time, so she settled for second best. While still in her teens she became a striptease artiste in a Budapest nightclub. By Hungarian standards she was earning good money. She needed every penny of it to pay for the monthly hospital bills for her mother's treatment.'

Leigh had never felt so ashamed. 'Why hadn't she told him all this.' He remembered picking up the photograph in Suki's flat, of the old lady with the clear bright eyes, 'She looks a fine woman,' he had said.

'She is,' Suki had replied.

'Are you listening, Simon?' Levenson asked.

Leigh nodded, and Levenson continued.

'One night the General, who was at that time in charge of the Secret Police in Hungary, came to the club where Suki was performing, with one of his mistresses. He was so taken by her that when the show was over after sending his mistress home, he went backstage to meet her.

'This part of the information was the most difficult to obtain,' added Levenson looking up.

Leigh nodded impatiently, waiting for

what was to come.

'I understand,' Levenson continued, 'that the General offered the girl a regular sum of money far in excess of her salary at the club, to give up her job and become his mistress.

'Suki, who up to that time had been a virgin, had to agree. Her mother had now been discharged from hospital and the girl was finding it increasingly more difficult to pay for the medicine and special foods that her mother needed, apart from the rent and other essentials of living. She would have done anything for her mother and pride is not a very valuable commodity under those circumstances,' Levenson added catching sight of the look of disgust on Leigh's face.

Leigh felt physically sick at the thought of the General's cold manicured hands touching Suki's beautiful body. If only she had told him. What he would or could have done he did not know, but now it was too late: Suki was dead and he would never have the chance to make up to her the years of hell and misery she must have gone through to keep and look after her mother. For the first time since he had been a small boy, Simon Leigh felt tears pricking at the back of his eyes.

'The worst is to come I'm afraid, Simon,' said Levenson pausing. Leigh pretended to blow his nose and fought to regain his self-control; when he replaced his handkerchief in his pocket his eyes were still moist.

'After a while the General tired of Suki, as he did all his mistresses. An all-purpose female agent was required at that time by the Communists in Brussels, so he sent her to the Moscow Spy School to be trained for two years, and then on to Brussels. He told her before she left Budapest, that if she ever once let them down or tried to doublecross them in any way, her mother would be killed. If she did her job well and conscientiously, her mother would receive the very best medical attention and would be well cared for.'

Levenson went on speaking for some time but Leigh was not listening. If he had known when he was in East Berlin what he knew now, he would have found some other way of killing the General. Levenson had been right when he had said, 'The cigar is much too good a death for him.'

'Are you listening, Simon?' Levenson said, when he saw that Leigh's attention seemed to be anywhere but in this room.

Leigh snapped himself back to face the man across the desk.

'Listen to me, Harold,' he said, striving to keep his voice under control. 'Before I went to Brussels you told me that we were fighting a war. At that time I neither believed nor really understood you. Now I both believe and understand.' He paused before going on.

'I want to join your army and fight.' His voice was now exaggeratedly calm and his eyes held a wildness that Levenson did not like.

'Simon,' he said, putting the folder down on the desk. 'Don't let your emotions conquer your reason. You'll have to think about this very carefully.'

'I don't want to think about anything,' said Leigh standing up. 'Either you want me and can use me, or you don't. If you don't, I'll wage my own private war. How I'll do it I don't know, but I'll never sleep soundly again knowing that such vermin exist in this world and that I'm doing nothing to try and exterminate them.'

Levenson was a shrewd judge of character and he had foreseen just such an outburst from Leigh. But its vehemence surprised him. He realized, not for the first time, that he would not like Simon Leigh for an enemy. A man full of hate with nothing to lose is the most dangerous animal on God's earth.

'Simon,' he said at last, 'in this war we're waging, there's no place for emotion or private vendettas. Unfortunately we can't afford such everyday luxuries. There's too much at stake for us to engage the wrong personnel. If you were to join us, you would have to become completely detached and uninvolved. This would not be easy for you. If you are really serious about this, we'll meet a month from now and if you can honestly tell me then that you are detached and uninvolved, we'll talk again.'

Leigh left the building soon afterwards, without seeing Gorebain again. Levenson escorted him to the lift.

At the lift doors, he put his hand on Leigh's shoulder.

'Simon, if you take my advice, you'll go away for a few weeks. Go to Cannes or Monte Carlo and get some sun and rest. Forget everything. You've been under a terrific strain lately and the best cure for you at the moment is plenty of sunshine and relaxation.'

'It's not such a bad idea,' thought Leigh bitterly, as the lift ascended rapidly to the ground floor. But he knew that he would not be going away.

He drove down Park Lane and was back in his flat ten minutes after leaving Levenson's office.

Immediately he telephoned his own office and asked for Joyce.

'Donald, I won't be coming back to the factory today. I want to discuss something with you. Can you meet me at my flat for a drink later this evening.'

'Certainly, Mr Leigh, what time?'

'Make it about eight.'

'I'll be there.'

Joyce's new found power as a director of the Company had not gone to his head. He was still the same level headed unflappable technician he had always been. It had been a shock to him, as it had everybody else at the factory, when he had first learned about Leigh's car accident in Germany.

He had telephoned St George's Hospital and asked if he could visit him, but they had said that he was not yet well enough to receive visitors.

When Leigh had returned to the office, he had seemed at first different somehow. Outwardly he was the same man, but there was something about him that was different. He was in some way less positive, less dynamic than the Simon Leigh who had left for Brussels a few weeks before.

But after a couple of weeks, he had returned to his normal forceful self and Donald Joyce, who had been genuinely concerned about him had relaxed.

Joyce did not often see Leigh socially and he always enjoyed it when he did.

Not that the conversation ever strayed far from the business.

At seven o'clock as he drove out of the factory gates in his new Rover 2000 he wondered what Leigh had to say to him that could not wait until morning.

14

Say Ahh!

Simon Leigh had decided before he left Levenson's office. It was in many ways a heartbreaking decision to reach, but he knew that if he gave himself too much time to think about it he might easily change his mind.

As soon as he had finished speaking to Donald Joyce, Leigh telephoned the London Office of the Anglo Affiliated Computer Corporation and asked for Edward Cantrell, the Managing Director.

'What name is it?' asked the efficient female voice on the other end of the line.

'Simon Leigh.'

Within a surprisingly short space of time the anglicized drawl of Edward D. Cantrell was asking Leigh how he was and where he had been lately.

Cantrell was a shrewd product of the Harvard Business School. He was a dedicated Corporation man in every sense of the word, and although not yet thirty already had some notable successes under his belt. He was a prominent figure in the British Electronics industry and the newspapers amicably referred to him as 'The Whizz Kid'; a description which strongly appealed to him. The only quality by which Edward D. Cantrell judged his fellow man was the state of his bank balance, and the only value he held precious was financial success.

Leigh, as a highly successful self-made man was 'in' on both counts, and Cantrell held tremendous admiration for him. When Leigh had rejected Anglo Affiliated's takeover bid some months previously, although bitterly disappointed as this would have been a further feather in his cap, Cantrell had understood Leigh's reasons. The welfare of his employees had been one of the main deterrents to Leigh's selling out, and although by American standards this was soft, Cantrell knew that in normal business negotiations, Leigh was as tough as any American.

'To what do I owe the pleasure of this

phone call, Mr Leigh?' Cantrell asked.

'I may be prepared to reconsider your Company's offer,' Leigh replied without preamble, lighting a slim Schimmelpenninck and inhaling deeply, something he never generally did.

There was a slight pause at the other end of the line. Leigh could imagine Cantrell rubbing his hands together with satisfaction.

'When can we meet, Mr Leigh,' he asked almost too eagerly.

'10 o'clock tomorrow morning, in my office,' Leigh answered, replacing the receiver.

★ ★ ★

For once the Friday evening traffic on the motorway was light. As Leigh pushed the accelerator hard down against the floor, the Bristol seemed to take off as it hit 60 miles in eight seconds. Quit when you're on top he thought wryly to himself.

Fifteen minutes previously he had driven out of the Factory gates for the last time. Tomorrow he was driving down to the wilds of Dorset to begin a new life.

Leigh Industrial Components Limited was now a subsidiary of the Anglo Affiliated Computer Corporation and Simon Leigh had relinquished all interests in the company, financial and otherwise. He had given up everything he had struggled and fought to build and felt a genuine sense of loss.

At the informal farewell party he had given, the staff had presented him with a miniature scale replica of the first computer that the firm had marketed. He had been more moved by this gesture than he would have admitted and when the three cheers for the 'Guvnor' had died down, he had held up his hand for silence in the large despatch bay where all the staff were assembled.

'I would like to thank you all for this,' he had begun holding up the replica computer. 'It means more to me than anything else you could have possibly given me.'

Leigh looked around the familiar faces that he had seen nearly every day for the past few years.

'I'd also like to thank you for your loyalty and hard work. I know that it has not always been easy, having to work all hours of the day and night to get an export order ready on time, but you have never once let me down and I'm proud of you all.

'As you know, Mr Joyce will be taking over here as Managing Director and I have a firm promise from the Directors of Anglo Affiliated Computers, who are taking this Company over that they will interfere as little as possible with the day-to-day running of the business or with the employing of personnel which will still be done internally.'

Leigh had heard from Joyce that a lot of the staff were worried that they would lose their jobs as a result of the take-over and he was anxious to reassure them. Rumours as to why he was leaving were rife. The most popularly accepted suggestion was that his car accident in East Germany was in some way responsible for his decision.

Perhaps the Guvnor wanted to take things easy now. He'd had enough tragedy in his life, one way and another. He was still young, and had plenty of money. Good luck to him if he wanted to sit back and enjoy the fruits of his success.

Donald Joyce knew there must be more to it than this but he said nothing, knowing that Leigh would tell him when he was good and ready. Leigh, of course, could not tell Joyce or anyone else, his real reasons for selling out, but he owed the man who had been with him from the first difficult days, some sort of explanation.

Half an hour before the farewell party, he had called Joyce into his office.

'Donald, you'll naturally be wondering why I've changed my mind so soon and sold out. Well, I'm afraid it was a simple matter of hard cash. They offered me too much money to refuse.'

Simon Leigh had in fact received three-quarters of a million pounds in shares and cash for his business, so to anybody who knew him less well, this would have been a more than convincing explanation for his selling out, but

Donald Joyce did know Leigh. He also knew his philosophy about the creating and building of a business being more important than the pure money side.

No, there was some other reason that Leigh was keeping to himself. Joyce knew that Simon Leigh was not the sort of man to sit on his bottom all day doing nothing and with all his money he was too intelligent to spend the rest of his life leading a playboy's existence, jetsetting around the playgrounds of the world.

Donald Joyce was not an eloquent man but in those few minutes alone with the man he admired almost to the point of hero worship, he had tried to express his gratitude for everything that Leigh had done for him.

'Mr Leigh,' he had said, 'you can give a man fifty thousand quid and he can spend it in a year; what you've given me is something precious, something money can't buy. You gave me opportunity when no one else would and I want to thank you for that from the bottom of my heart.'

Leigh forced Joyce's words to the back

of his mind and angrily accelerated past a chauffeur driven Bentley which had been selfishly hogging the fast lane.

Tonight he was not worried about speed cops: at 120 m.p.h. he still had plenty in reserve, but out of deference to the indignant little salesman who had to pull his Cortina out of the Bristol's way when he was doing the legal maximum, Leigh did not increase his speed any further.

Before leaving the Factory he had shaken hands with everybody, from Joyce down to the girl who looked after the laundry.

When he came to Janine, his secretary, who although superficially cool and poised had been head over heels in love with Leigh since the first week she had come to work for him, he was surprised to find her sniffling into a minute handkerchief. He was surprised, because although attractive and desirable, Janine had always been so efficient and business like in her relations towards him that he had often felt that she did not much like him. He had playfully kissed her on the cheek, which only served to make her weeping worse.

He had given instructions that every member of the staff was to receive two weeks extra wages in their pay packet at the end of the week which he was paying out of his own pocket.

As he was walking over to his car at the end of the party, he had been both amused and touched to overhear one hard bitten old boy, who acted as nightwatchman, remark to a companion.

'The Guvnor may be a bit of a 'ard nut, but he's the best bleedin' boss I've ever worked for.'

His companion had nodded vigorously in agreement.

Leigh slowed to come off the motorway. He was determined to put his business, his ex-business, behind him. There was the all important future to consider.

★ ★ ★

He had been to see Harold Levenson a week previously and had discussed with

280

him the financial arrangements he had made with Anglo Affiliated Computers.

Levenson's trimmed eyebrows had knitted together in a frown.

'Simon,' he said. 'You don't need me to tell you that financially, you've done an excellent deal, but you haven't done this for the money, have you?'

Before Leigh could answer he had continued.

'You're relying too much on being accepted by our 'organization'. Just suppose you're turned down, what will you do then?'

Leigh had looked at the fat Chief of the Secret Service.

'Harold,' he said, 'I've passed the point of no return. If I am turned down I'll wage my own private war.'

'Simon, that's a stupid, childish idea.' Levenson protested angrily. The terrible thing was, he knew that Leigh was absolutely serious. He was that type of man.

Leigh had smiled suddenly. 'Let's stop talking as if I'd already been rejected. You told me I had to become detached and uninvolved. Well, here I am, detached and uninvolved. What's the next step?'

Levenson had shrugged resignedly.

'Simon, I can't give you a definite yes or no.'

'So where do I go from here?' he had persisted.

Levenson seemed to make up his mind about something.

He picked up one of the three black telephones from his desk. 'Get me Dr Silveman on the line.'

There was a short pause, then Levenson was speaking into the telephone.

'Hello, David, how are you?

'I'm fine. I'm sending a business colleague along to see you. I want you to give him a thorough examination.

'Yes, I'm considering putting him on the Executive Board of Display Advertising and I want to make sure that he's 100 per cent fit to undergo the training scheme. His name's Leigh. Simon Leigh.

'Fine, I'll tell him you're expecting him. Goodbye David.'

Leigh had gone straight from Connaught Place to Dr Silveman's surgery, having arranged to go back and see Levenson at 4 o'clock the following day, by which time his medical report should have come through from the doctor who was retained as official Medical Adviser to British Intelligence.

Dr Silveman's surgery was in a small mews behind Wimpole Street and Leigh had some difficulty finding a parking place.

The doctor had answered the door himself. He was a middle-aged, ruddy complexioned man with a head of thick white hair; he reminded Leigh very much of the typical cartoon character of the absent minded professor with his slight stoop and metal framed glasses: but there the resemblance ended.

There was nothing vague about Dr Silveman. His eyes were perceptive and clear behind the glasses and his handshake firm.

'Come in, Mr Leigh,' the doctor said in a strong foreign accent. 'I understand you're thinking of joining Mr Levenson's board?'

Leigh, who was fast familiarizing himself with Secret Service double talk, told the doctor that he was not thinking of joining, but as far as he was concerned he was going to join, unless, of course, he was prevented by his medical.

The doctor gave a dry chuckle and led him into a small surgery, fitted with equipment and gadgets which Leigh had never seen before.

A girl of no more than twenty-four, was standing by the window pouring some amber liquid into a test tube, she smiled at Leigh as he followed the doctor into his room.

'My assistant, Miss Powell,' said the doctor.

Leigh returned the girl's smile. She was not very tall, but what she lacked in size was made up in other ways. Her body was firm and supple under the white overall and her hazel eyes were full of fun and laughter. She wore her long, fair hair in a ponytail and Leigh wondered idly what she looked like with her hair down and her clothes off.

'Please undress, Mr Leigh,' said the doctor, taking some instruments from a drawer.

Leigh looked from the girl to the doctor.

'I assure you, Mr Leigh,' said the doctor gravely, 'that you have nothing that Miss Powell has not seen many times before.'

Leigh looked from the doctor to the girl who gave him a mischievous wink.

This did nothing to encourage him and as he grudgingly took off his clothes, he saw the girl was grinning with unconcealed enjoyment at his discomfort.

The grin left her face when she saw the still fresh scars on his chest and back.

The doctor, who had seen many such scars and worse, made no comment but proceeded to give Leigh the most thorough medical examination to which he had ever been subjected.

He was with the doctor for nearly three hours and when he left the surgery he felt as if no part of his body was any longer his own.

Miss Powell had immediately become serious and professional when the doctor had began his examination, always making sure that he had the right instrument in his hand. Also she made notes which the doctor dictated throughout the examination.

Towards the end of the examination Leigh had been instructed to swing from a metal bar across the ceiling while the doctor went all over his body with a stethoscope.

The girl had winked at him again while he was swinging, and he had been sorely tempted to jump down from the bar and go over and spank her.

At last when it was over and he was dressed again the doctor had left the room to make a telephone call. Leigh looked at the girl who was sterilizing some instruments.

'I'll teach you to laugh at a poor defenceless man in the nude,' he had said, and going over had kissed her firmly on the lips, having decided this would achieve more than a spanking.

The girl was so astonished that she had made no move to resist and when the doctor returned a few minutes later, he was surprised to find that Leigh was now grinning and Miss Powell looked as though she was suffering some embarrassment.

★ ★ ★

The next day Leigh had been five minutes early for his appointment with Levenson and at the now familiar house in Connaught Place, he went through the usual ritual before gaining admittance to Levenson's office.

Levenson had looked stern when Leigh entered and did not give him the usual greeting.

Leigh wondered, with concern, what had caused the black looks this afternoon.

'Simon, I'm surprised at you,' Levenson had begun.

Leigh frowned in surprise.

'I've just had Dr Silveman on the phone. Apparently you tried to rape his poor assistant, while he was out of the room for five minutes yesterday.'

Leigh stood speechless for several seconds.

Then Levenson began to roar with laughter, and Leigh who had thought for a moment that the man was being serious, had relaxed and laughed with him. It was the first time that he had ever seen Levenson really laugh.

Soon Levenson had become serious. He pointed to some sheets of foolscap lying on his desk.

'Simon, this report on your general health is all right, but to be of any use to us, you'll have to cut down considerably on your drinking. Also, you don't take nearly enough exercise.'

At these words Leigh had felt light-headed and happy. Here was the first positive indication that he had not been turned down.

'You will also have to go back to school for six months,' Levenson had continued.

'Go back to school!' Leigh had exclaimed, wondering if this was another joke.

But Levenson's flabby face remained serious.

'Yes, Spy School. It's in Dorset, near Bridport. Nice place. Georgian house standing in 300 acres of private wood-land. If you think training for the

Commandos was tough, let me tell you, that out of 200 personnel that pass through the school annually, only nine per cent stay the course.'

'If you're trying to put me off, you're wasting your breath, Harold,' Leigh had replied.

'I'm not trying to put you off at all, Simon, just trying to warn you. Because you go to spy school does not automatically mean that you'll stay the course. And if you should drop out, there's no question of a second chance.'

'I won't drop out,' Leigh had replied, matter of factly.

'No, Simon. I don't believe you will.'

Levenson had risen from behind his desk and Leigh stood up to go.

'I'll talk to you about salaries and expenses when you return from Dorset. I've arranged for you to go down on Saturday.'

He handed Leigh a long buff envelope.

'Directions how to find the place, also a guide to what to take with you. Memorize the contents then burn them.'

'I don't want any salary for this,' Leigh

said taking the envelope. 'I'm doing it because I want to.'

'I've told you before, Simon, we can't afford personal vendettas in this business. If you're accepted you will be paid along with everybody else, myself included. If your conscience bothers you, give the money to charity.'

Leigh had shrugged and put the envelope in his breast pocket.

'What do I learn at this school?' he asked as the two men left the basement office.

Levenson had walked with him to the lift and when he spoke, his voice was as matter of fact as if he was reciting the itinerary for a summer holiday.

'The first two months are spent learning to kill efficiently and quickly with various weapons. That is followed by a months training in sabotage, code breaking and communications, and the last three months are spent in practical training.'

'What happens at the end of the six months?' Leigh asked, stepping into the small lift.

'If you pass the course, you'll be sent before a Selection Committee composed of myself and four others to decide which sector of the Secret Service you can best serve. If it's decided to make you a full-time operational agent, you'll be sent on your first mission within a very short while. But I warn you, Simon, even if you are accepted, a lot of the job is routine paper work between missions.'

Leigh knew as he left Connaught Place that he had now really reached the point of no return. As he started the Bristol, he wondered what Klaire would have thought about this new and totally foreign way of life he had chosen for himself.

'From a businessman to a spy in ten easy lessons.' He smiled to himself as he swung the Bristol into Edgware Road.

15

Second Time Lucky

As Simon Leigh packed his Revelation for the second time in two months, he felt like a schoolboy on the last day of the holidays.

Like a schoolboy he was determined to get the most out of his last night of freedom and was in two minds whether to get blind drunk in some club or go and play chemmy at Crockfords and only get a little drunk.

Over the last few days, as well as tying up business matters, he had worked non-stop putting his private affairs in order and his accountant, with whom he had lunched during the week had made the observation that Leigh could afford to live for the rest of his life at the rate of £25,000 a year without ever having to work again.

Leigh had smiled at the accountant,

who was an old friend and had replied, 'Stephen, I can only smoke one cigar at a time, drive one Rolls Royce at a time and drink one bottle of champagne at a time, so whether I live at the rate of twenty, fifty, or five hundred thousand pounds a year, it would make no difference.'

When Leigh had finished packing, he poured out a large whisky. As he sat drinking and thinking, he suddenly realized that he did not want to be alone, tonight of all nights. Tonight was very special to him; it was the symbolic end to an old life, the beginning of a new one. The whisky was not bucking him up as it usually did and it struck him, not for the first time since Klaire's death how very lonely he was with all his money.

'I'm not going to spend tonight alone,' he decided as he poured out his third large Scotch.

Klaire, Suki, that was the past. He would never forget his wife, whom he had adored, nor his Suki, whom he now believed had loved him and whom he had known for less than a week.

Since East Berlin, Leigh had come to

realize that his self-imposed martyrdom with regard to women was futile and meaningless. Klaire would not have wished it and he was not proving anything to himself or anyone else. He knew now that there has to come a time when a man stops living in the past and starts to live once more for the present and future.

He looked at his watch, six-thirty-five. On a sudden impulse he dialled Dr Silveman's number hoping it was not too late.

A female voice, young and self-assured, answered.

'Dr Silveman's surgery.'

Leigh smiled at the thought of the expression on her face when he had kissed her.

'Hello, Miss Powell. This is the man who seemed to amuse you so much the other afternoon with his antics in the nude.'

Leigh could visualize the girl's mischievous smile the other end.

'Hello, Mr Leigh. What can I do for you? If you want the doctor, I'm afraid he's away at a conference and won't be back until Monday morning.'

'I don't want the doctor, I want you. Will you have dinner with me tonight. I'm going away tomorrow.'

'Yes, I know you are,' she replied.

Leigh wondered how much else she knew.

'Well, Mr Leigh, I'm not sure that it's at all ethical to see patients socially,' she teased.

Leigh smiled.

'I appreciate that, Miss Powell, but the thing is I need some therapeutic treatment and as the doctor is not there to give it to me, I'm afraid I'll have to make do with you.'

She laughed. It was a provocative, exciting sound.

'All right, Mr Leigh. In the interests of medicine and your health, I will cancel all my other engagements for this evening and have dinner with you.'

'Good. Tell me where you live and I'll pick you up about nine.'

Carine Powell had read Leigh's case history, which at Levenson's request, St George's Hospital had passed on to Dr

Silveman. Although she had been prepared to see scars on his body, she had
been genuinely shocked by the extent and
nature of them. The doctor had told her
afterwards that they should all fade in
time, but nevertheless it must have been
some beating he had taken.

In her three years with the doctor, she
had seen many men with scars and
wounds far worse than Leigh's, yet for
some reason she had been more affected
by him than any of the others. There was
something hard and uncompromising
about the lean face under the dark brown
hair that had made a deep impression on
her. He was the sort of man that she
could visualize sitting in some bar
drinking alone and brooding. A loner, not
prepared to give himself completely to
anyone. Looking into Simon Leigh's eyes
when he had kissed her so unexpectedly,
she had seen an elusiveness, a coldness:
but somehow in complete contradiction
to this, she felt instinctively that the man
had a hidden warmth under his hard
exterior which he was frightened to show.

She never knew a great deal about the

men that passed through the doctor's hands, but she was old and intelligent enough to realize that it would be very wrong and very foolish to ever allow herself to become involved with any of them and she began to regret accepting Leigh's invitation the moment he had rung off the phone.

It was so easy to get to like people, only to find out one day that they had disappeared while on a 'business trip' abroad. In her training she had been warned very strongly about becoming involved with any of the doctor's patients.

'It's not fair on yourself or them,' the man at the training college had said.

But from what she gathered from Leigh's case history, he was not yet an agent and his medical was merely to ascertain his suitability for undergoing training.

'But then, if he was not an agent, where did those vicious scars come from,' she wondered. 'No car crash ever caused those sort of injuries.'

At ten minutes past nine, the doorbell of her tiny flat in South Kensington rang and as she looked at herself in the hall mirror before answering it, she knew it was too late to worry about whether she had done the right thing or not. The die was cast. Que sera sera.

As soon as she opened the door and saw Simon Leigh's green eyes searching her face she was glad that she had accepted, come what may.

'Hello, Miss Powell.'

'Hello, Mr Leigh.'

She gave a cry of delight when she saw Leigh's car, the metallic paintwork glistening under a street lamp.

'What a super car. Is it a Jensen?'

'No, a Bristol.' Leigh loved the enthusiasm with which the girl showed her feelings.'

'Most British girls,' he thought, 'make such an act of trying to appear cool and unimpressed by everything, that it makes a refreshing change to find a girl both genuine and uninhibited.'

He had booked a table at the 21 Club for dinner, but he wanted to have a drink at the Dorchester Bar first. He was not usually in the least bit sentimental, but for some reason, he thought it would be lucky for him to drink tonight, where everything had begun.

Driving down Brompton Road he looked at the girl's reflection in his driving mirror and said,

'I'm not going to go on calling you Miss Powell all evening, you know.'

Her hazel eyes met his in the mirror and smiled.

'My name is Carine.'

After a couple of drinks at the Dorchester, they walked the few yards to the 21 Club, each excited by the other's company, both looking forward to the evening ahead.

When the second bottle of Chateau neuf du Pape was being uncorked, Carine squeezed Leigh's hand under the table.

'In a purely medical capacity, Simon, I must advise you to cut down on your drinking.'

Although she spoke in a jocular tone she meant this advice seriously. She knew from the doctor's report and Leigh's answers to some of his questions that Leigh drank heavily, but the amount of alcohol that he had consumed both before and during dinner concerned her.

'Don't worry,' he smiled, refilling both their glasses. 'Tonight for me is a final fling. A fond farewell to La Dolce Vita.'

'I doubt it, somehow,' she said almost sadly, looking into his eyes and raising her glass in a silent toast.

Leigh wanted to ask her about her job with Doctor Silveman, but he knew that this would not be fair and that she could not tell him anyway. He was interested to learn how a girl so young could become involved even in the periphery of this business; but then Suki was not so old, he remembered bitterly.

'What time do you leave tomorrow?' Carine asked sensing that his thoughts were far away.

'About ten in the morning,' Leigh replied, pouring cream down the back of his spoon into the black coffee.

'You don't want to have too late a night then,' she said.

'No, nurse. Of course not. But let's have one last drink before we go.'

'No,' Carine said firmly. 'Apart from

your health, God help you if some keen policeman stops you with a breathalyser while you're driving.'

Leigh laughed at her for once serious face, and they left the club soon afterwards, without the final drink.

Walking back to the car she took his arm and neither of them spoke until they reached the Bristol.

'I know a club,' said Leigh, opening the car door, 'where there are no licencing laws, where they serve the best coffee in London and where only personal friends of mine are admitted.'

'Really,' replied Carine, raising her eyebrows in mock gravity. 'This I've got to see.'

They did not speak for several minutes: Carine desperately wanted to preserve the lighthearted atmosphere of the evening but she knew that Simon Leigh's thoughts could never be far away from tomorrow.

'There must be a long waiting list for membership of this club,' she said as the Bristol swept majestically round Sloane Square.'

'Oh, there is,' Leigh replied, seriously. 'Some nights there are queues of people at the door stretching a hundred yards.'

'All female, of course.'

'Naturally.'

When they pulled up at the block of flats in Lower Sloane Street, Carine pretended to be surprised and angry.

'You 'orrible man, luring me back to yer flat under false pretences and me a poor innocent girl oop from the country, wot doesn't know no better.'

As they kissed in the lift, for once Leigh did not curse the length of time it took to reach the ninth floor.

After looking round his flat, Carine made Turkish coffee in the percolator, while Leigh poured out two large brandies.

They talked of frivolous, meaningless things and during one of several prolonged silences Leigh took Carine's hand and led her into the bedroom. Drawing the curtains, he took her into his arms and held her very tightly to him.

But she pulled herself free from his embrace and sat down on the bed.

'Simon,' she said, her face suddenly serious. 'Are you using me? I mean because you're going away tomorrow, do you just want someone to make love to, to tell you you're doing the right thing and that everything is going to be fine. Is that why we've had this evening?'

Leigh remembered how a few hours earlier he had decided he could not be alone tonight. Perhaps Carine was right, he did not know himself.

'What are you talking about?' said Leigh, sitting down beside her and taking her small hand in his.

'I'm talking about you, Simon. Tomorrow you're going off to learn how to kill, destroy and God knows what else.'

She could not stop herself now. The words gushed out in an uncontrollable torrent. 'Does your final fling tonight also include having me and then discarding me like a toy that you've grown tired of and no longer want?'

'Perhaps,' Leigh replied wearily letting go of her hand and lying back on the bed. 'Perhaps I don't really want anybody any more. Anyway let's be completely honest with each other, Carine. You don't want to become involved with me. It wouldn't be fair to either of us.'

'No,' she replied, looking straight ahead. 'We mustn't become involved with each other.'

She remained silent for a few minutes, then she spoke again.

'You know, Simon, I don't really think you are using me. You just won't admit, even to yourself, that you're human and need somebody like everybody else.'

As she unbuttoned his shirt, she asked him the question that she had been determined not to ask.

'Simon, how did you get those dreadful scars all over your chest and back.'

Leigh lifted her chin and kissed her lightly on the nose.

'I fell off my bicycle,' he said.

Later, much later, Simon Leigh awoke to find Carine, wearing only his towelling bathrobe, setting down a tray of coffee on the bedside table beside him.

She smiled and bending down kissed him on the forehead.

'What time is it?' he asked.

She looked at her watch. 'Three o'clock.'

'Three o'clock in the morning,' he repeated. 'What a wonderful time to be lying in bed drinking coffee with a beautiful girl.'

'I shouldn't ask this question and, of course, you needn't, Simon,' she said, getting back into bed beside him, 'answer it, but what makes a man like you, young, highly successful, with apparently everything to live for, want to go off and train to become a professional spy, a paid killer, with a pretty good chance of being killed yourself within a year?'

'That's a good question,' Leigh answered with a smile. 'But as you said, I don't have to answer it, and I'm not sure that I could anyway.' He lied.

Carine knew that she would not learn any more from Simon Leigh; it was wrong of her to question him. She had to accept that this must be strictly a one night stand for both of them.

She finished her coffee and turning off the bedside light came into his arms. She clung tightly to him, trying to hold back the tears that were pricking her eyes.

When Simon Leigh awoke again, the Rolex at the side of his bed, showed twenty-past-seven. There was no sign of Carine and her clothes were gone. As he was putting on his bathrobe, which she had left on the bed, he found a piece of paper sticking out of the pocket. The writing was feminine and rather childish.

'Darling Simon,
   'I didn't want to disturb you when you were sleeping so peacefully, so I crept out. Thanks a million for the dinner and everything, it was wonderful.

   As you said, neither of us really wanted to get involved and although for you it was probably just like two ships passing in the night, I want you to know that I will never forget you.

   Take care of yourself, darling, and go easy on the booze and La Dolce Vita.
                    All love,
                    Carine.'

Leigh read the letter twice, and then carefully he tore it into small pieces.

After a long shower, Leigh dressed unhurriedly, in a navy cashmere sweater, sand coloured twill trousers and an old suede jacket that Klaire had given him.

By nine-thirty he was ready to leave; with a final glance around the flat he would not be seeing for six months, Leigh clicked his suitcase shut.

He drove slowly out to the Staines By-pass and on to the A.30. He was expected in Bridport about two o'clock, but Levenson had told him not to kill himself getting there.

'After all, Simon,' he had said, with a brief smile, 'you'll be buried in the depths of Dorset for the next six months, so another hour or so either way, won't make much difference.'

It was an overcast, miserable day and the traffic out of London was heavy, but after Hartley Wintney, it thinned out and Leigh did not let the Bristol's speedometer slip much below seventy until he slowed to come into Basingstoke.

A few miles the other side of

Basingstoke, a white convertible Mercedes 280 SL with the hood down pulled out of a lay by and cruised up behind the Bristol. Instead of overtaking, however, it seemed content to sit on Leigh's tail, always maintaining a safe distance from the back of the Bristol.

By the time he passed through Sutton Scodney, Leigh was becoming increasingly irritated with the driver of the German car, who accelerated every time the Bristol increased speed and slowed down whenever Leigh braked, never making any attempt to pass him. Leigh was not usually an intolerant driver, but the strange behaviour of the Mercedes was beginning to unnerve him, and he made up his mind to shake the white car off his tail before he really lost his temper. As he manoeuvred the Bristol round a sharp curve in the road and up a steep incline, without warning he kicked down on the accelerator and shot away from the Mercedes so fast that he was forced hard back against the Bristol's padded upholstery. As the Bristol reached the top of the hill, Leigh glanced down at the speedometer; already the needle was registering 85 m.p.h. But the driver of the Mercedes had obviously been anticipating just such a move; with a superbly executed racing change, the powerful white car roared up behind him, its twin exhausts rising to an orgasmic crescendo before the driver changed up into top.

A sharp double bend was ahead and Leigh knew that it would be madness to maintain his present speed, but by now the Mercedes was so close on his tail that to touch his brakes would send the Mercedes crashing into the back of him. Cursing his pursuer for making him drive so recklessly and praying that the new radial ply tyres he had had fitted would work the wonders claimed from them, Leigh kept his foot hard down on the accelerator as the bend rushed up to meet him.

Miraculously the precise power assisted steering took all the punishment that he inflicted on it as at nearly 100 m.p.h., Leigh desperately swung the steering wheel over to the left and hardly before the wheels could change direction, forced it savagely back to the right. At first the tyres despite their screeching, gripped the smooth road surface, but as the Bristol came roaring out of the bend, the speedometer needle flickering around the hundred and five mark, Leigh felt his tail begin to go.

The road was still curving sharply to the left and to touch his brakes now would inevitably send the Bristol into a skid, but the Mercedes was not a car's length behind him and sweat pouring down his ashen face, Simon Leigh forced his foot to remain pressed down on the accelerator pedal as the car began to spin madly out of control. Then the bend was behind him, and the Bristol was careering erratically down the wrong side of a straight, but narrow stretch of road; mercifully no cars were coming the other way: gently Leigh touched the brake pedal. Gradually, reluctantly, the big car was coaxed out of its crazy skid and back into control.

The squat Mercedes, with its superb roadholding came shrieking out of the bend not ten yards behind him, its tyres screaming protest, but not losing their adhesion.

The white car was so close to the Bristol that Leigh, glancing into his mirror, could see the driver's face clearly framed. The man was wearing a large pair of sunglasses, and all Leigh could see of his face was a long, bulbous nose and a small, mean mouth puckered into a pout of concentration. Also strangely, although not old, the man was completely bald. As Leigh once more pulled away from the white Mercedes, he had a strange feeling in the back of his mind that the bald-headed man reminded him of someone.

But he did not have time to try and remember who it was; already the strong, clean lines of the car behind were once more becoming larger in his mirror. As he slowed to negotiate a double bend, Leigh knew without knowing why that there was more to the bald man's suicidal driving than a desire to prove his Mercedes faster than the Bristol. This was more than a foolhardy race between two extremely fast

311

and potent cars. As once more the Mercedes closed up on him, Leigh knew that he was driving for more than the pride of proving his Bristol superior to the Mercedes: a cold knot of fear mingled with anger gripped his stomach as he realized that he was driving for his life.

Hurtling the responsive Bristol up hills and round bends, Leigh had no time to permit the fear to take hold of him. His concentration was fully occupied trying to keep the car on the road. He knew that the Bristol could leave the six cylinder Mercedes on the straight, but with the German car's swing axle rear suspension, the sharper bends would present a different proposition. Both cars had fantastic suspension developed from their racing heritage and Leigh knew as he held tightly on to the wheel that it was going to be a question of sheer driving skill.

As Leigh braked once more to come into a tortuous double bend, he shot a glance into his right wing mirror. The Mercedes, which he had temporarily out-paced, was now close on his tail again, and with its tenacious road holding would out-accelerate him on the approaching bend. Leigh was already pushing the Bristol round the twisting road too fast, but the white car was right behind him. It began to pull out to the right and Leigh bit deep into his lip, oblivious to pain, as he threw the Bristol into the last sharp shoulder of the bend. The Mercedes was still accelerating and both cars were now doing well over ninety miles an hour.

'So the bastard is going to try and take me on the bend.' Leigh forced himself not to take his foot off the accelerator as the two cars tore round the bend, leaving behind on the road, black rubber shreds from their tortured tyres.

The Mercedes was on the wrong side of the road and the driver was desperately trying to draw level with the Bristol. With amazing skill he brought the white car up beside the Bristol: as the two cars raced out of the bend, both parallel to one another as if joined by an invisible wire, it suddenly struck Leigh who it was the bald man reminded him of . . .

The two cars flashed out of the bend as one, inches separating them: Leigh turned his head to see if he dared increase his speed. As he turned, the bald man raised the Luger he had been holding and with his right hand frantically grappling with the steering wheel, aimed the gun through the side window of the Bristol at Leigh's head.

Instinctively, Leigh trod on his brakes and the bullet, which should have hit his temple, shattered the Bristol's laminated windscreen and buried itself harmlessly in the passenger seat. Leigh saw the bald man's face contorted in a gesture of anger and frustration when he saw that he had missed.

The Mercedes was now ahead, its boot level with the Bristol's bonnet. Leigh had a fleeting image of the bald man aiming over his shoulder in an attempt to get another shot, then the Mercedes, which must have been travelling by now at more than 100 m.p.h., mounted the offside kerb, somersaulted twice and burst into a sheet of orange flame.

When Leigh had brought the Bristol to a halt he pushed the broken glass through the shattered windscreen. He felt cold suddenly. Not from the air rushing in from where the windscreen had been, but cold inside, as if his blood had been iced.

Automatically, without thinking, he turned off the engine and opened the car door. Shivering, he walked the fifty yards back to what remained of the Mercedes: before he reached it he saw the bald man.

He had been thrown clear of the car and was lying spreadeagled across the roadside ten yards away from the smouldering wreckage of the Mercedes. Leigh could see without bending down that the man was dead.

Although he had been thrown clear when the Mercedes had first mounted the kerb, he had cracked his skull as he landed on the hard road surface. There was an air of horrific unreality about the smooth, bald head stained scarlet with blood. The man's sunglasses had shattered and a long sliver of tinted glass was protruding from one unseeing eye. The gun with which he had tried to kill Leigh was still gripped tightly in his left hand, as if even in death, he derived comfort and strength from it. Leigh knew that it would take a lot of strength to break that grip. A dead man's grip is like a vice.

Unhurriedly, Leigh returned to his own car. He sat there for a few moments without moving. A car passed and the driver stared curiously at the man sitting motionless in the Bristol with the shattered windscreen. Thankfully he did not stop to see if he could help, but it would not be long before some well meaning motorist summoned the police.

Leigh reached forward and picked up the telephone from beneath the dashboard. As he was giving the operator the number, he remembered that he had put a flask of whisky in the glove compartment before going to Brussels. He prayed that it was still there. Clumsily, his hand shaking uncontrollably, he fumbled with the key in the lock. When he found the flask he could not at first stop his hands trembling enough to unscrew the cap. When he took the flask away from his lips, his hands were no longer shaking and he had stopped shivering.

A female voice answered the number on the second ring, Leigh reclined his seat and in a voice which, thanks to the whisky, came out normal, asked to speak to the 'Chairman'.

Within seconds Levenson's familiar voice was on the line.

'What's the trouble, Simon?' Levenson had instructed Leigh only to use this number in cases of extreme emergency.

Leigh took another swig at the whisky flask before replying.

'When you told me not to kill myself getting to Dorset, you gave me good advice. My fictitious car accident in East Berlin has finally caught up with me.'

Briefly, he gave an account of his pursuit and attempted murder by the driver of the white Mercedes.

Levenson listened in silence to the description of the man now lying dead on the roadside. Then he confirmed Leigh's suspicions as to the identity of the bald-headed man.

When Simon Leigh had finished speaking to the 'Chairman' as Levenson would be known to him in the future, he opened the Bristol's passenger door and leaning out over the grass verge, he retched until his stomach felt as if it had been rent apart.

THE END

We do hope that you have enjoyed reading this large print book.

Did you know that all of our titles are available for purchase?

We publish a wide range of high quality large print books including:
Romances, Mysteries, Classics
General Fiction
Non Fiction and Westerns

Special interest titles available in large print are:
The Little Oxford Dictionary
Music Book, Song Book
Hymn Book, Service Book

Also available from us courtesy of Oxford University Press:
Young Readers' Dictionary
(large print edition)
Young Readers' Thesaurus
(large print edition)

For further information or a free brochure, please contact us at:
Ulverscroft Large Print Books Ltd.,
The Green, Bradgate Road, Anstey,
Leicester, LE7 7FU, England.
Tel: (00 44) **0116 236 4325**
Fax: (00 44) **0116 234 0205**

Other titles in the
Linford Mystery Library:

**TURN DOWN AN
EMPTY GLASS**

Basil Copper

L.A. private detective Mike Faraday is
plunged into a bizarre web of Haitian
voodoo and murder when the beautiful singer Jenny Lundquist comes to
him in fear for her life. Staked out at
the lonely Obelisk Point, Mike sees
the sinister Legba, the voodoo god of
the crossroads, with his cane and
straw sack. But Mike discovers that
beneath the superstition and an
apparently motiveless series of appall-
ing crimes is an ingenious plot — with
a multi-million dollar prize.